WEREWOLF RISING

WEREWOLF

RISING

R.L. LaFevers

DUTTON CHILDREN'S BOOKS

DUTTON CHILDREN'S BOOKS
A division of Penguin Young Readers Group

Published by the Penguin Group
Penguin Group (USA) Inc., 375 Hudson Street, New York, New York 10014, U.S.A. • Penguin Group (Canada), 90 Eglinton Avenue East, Suite 700, M4P 2Y3 (a division of Pearson Penguin Canada Inc.) • Penguin Books Ltd, 80 Strand, London WC2R 0RL, England • Penguin Ireland, 25 St Stephen's Green, Dublin 2, Ireland (a division of Penguin Books Ltd) • Penguin Group (Australia), 250 Camberwell Road, Camberwell, Victoria 3124, Australia (a division of Pearson Australia Group Pty Ltd) • Penguin Books India Pvt Ltd, 11 Community Centre, Panchsheel Park, New Delhi—110 017, India • Penguin Group (NZ), Cnr Airborne and Rosedale Roads, Albany, Auckland 1310, New Zealand (a division of Pearson New Zealand Ltd) • Penguin Books (South Africa) (Pty) Ltd, 24 Sturdee Avenue, Rosebank, Johannesburg 2196, South Africa • Penguin Books Ltd, Registered Offices: 80 Strand, London WC2R 0RL, England

The publisher does not have any control over and does not assume any responsibility for author or third-party websites of their content.

LIBRARY OF CONGRESS CATALOGING-IN-PUBLICATION DATA
La Fevers, R. L. (Robin L.)
Werewolf rising / R.L. LaFevers.
p. cm.
Summary: Just before his thirteenth birthday, an uncle he never knew takes Luc deep into the woods of the Pacific Northwest, where he learns that he is a werewolf whose pack is in danger from fanatics who are following his trail.
ISBN 0-525-47665-2
[1. Werewolves—Fiction. 2. Wolves—Fiction. 3. Uncles—Fiction. 4. Coming of age—Fiction. 5. Horror stories.] I. Title.

PZ7.L1414Wer 2006
[Fic]—dc22 2005023920

Published in the United States by Dutton Children's Books,
a division of Penguin Young Readers Group
345 Hudson Street, New York, New York 10014
www.penguin.com/youngreaders

Designed by Jason Henry
Printed in USA * First American Edition
1 3 5 7 9 10 2 6 4 2

To Erin Murphy,
who believed
and believed
and believed.

And to Lucia Monfried, Sarah Pope, and
Stephanie Owens Lurie, who believed some more.
When the right people believe in you, miracles can happen.

WEREWOLF RISING

1

I lay on my bed and felt the terrible thing lurking in my room draw closer. I strained to listen, but could hear nothing over the thundering of my heart. I trembled with fever. My body refused to obey my command to sit up, and see what was coming. My skin pulled and stretched, as if the terrible thing were calling it right off my bones. I shivered, both cold and hot at the same time. Somewhere deep inside, fear and anger swirled together in a tight clump, pressing against my chest and making me want to howl with pain and frustration.

And still it came closer.

I struggled to rise until my teeth ached with the strain of it. Finally, with a sound more like a growl than anything human, I wrenched myself up from the bed and found myself staring into the bloodshot eyes of a ravening beast.

And the beast was me.

I jerked upright as I tore myself out of the nightmare. My heart pounded in my chest, the sound of it filling my ears and blocking out all the other sounds of the night. I was drenched in sweat, my soaked T-shirt sticking to me like a thick layer of paste.

I threw off my covers, rubbed my eyes with my hands, and tried to remember how to breathe. I'd first had this dream almost a month ago, but it was coming more often now, almost every night this week.

Knowing I would need a few minutes to calm myself before I could go back to sleep, I crossed over to the window and perched on the sill. As I stared out over the bright lights of Seattle, thick gray clouds parted to let the moon shine through. It wasn't quite full, but it was big enough to fill my room with a pale silver light that made the shadows disappear.

2

It wasn't until I saw my fist slam into Brandon Blecker's face that I realized today was going to be different. Way different.

It was such a shock, seeing that fist come out of nowhere, that I looked over my shoulder to see who might have punched him. Usually, Blecker's the one doing the punching. And usually, he's punching me.

But not today. Today he sat in the dirt clutching his nose, glaring up at me with equal parts fury, fear, and surprise. Blood began to seep out from between his fingers, a deep red trickle that nearly hypnotized me. A strong coppery smell filled the air, making my nose twitch and my mouth water. I licked my lips.

I realized that my right hand was killing me, all the knuckles throbbing like I'd just jammed my fist into a cement wall. Joey slapped me on the shoulder. "Way to go, Luc!"

I turned to Joey in disbelief. "Me?" It came out in a

squeak that would have been embarrassing if I wasn't in shock.

"Yeah, you. Luc Never-Hit-Anybody-No-Matter-What Grayson!"

I glanced at the small crowd that was forming around us. "Want to say that a little louder, Joey?"

He threw back his head and laughed. "Welcome to the Playground Warriors Association." He glanced up. "Here comes Beecham, right on schedule. Don't worry. She and the vice principal will give you an official welcome into our ranks. Usually it's suspension, but since you're Mr. Perfect, it'll probably only be detention."

The yard duty strode toward us, her iron-gray hair frizzed out around her like a grizzly halo, the look on her face—not happy.

She reached us before I had a chance to think of a decent explanation. Puzzled, she stood over Brandon, hands on her hips, her head cocked to the side. "How'd you get down there, Blecker?"

Still holding his nose, Brandon pointed at me. "He did it."

She turned to me in obvious disbelief. "You trying to tell me that Grayson here knocked you on your butt?" Giving me the once-over, she asked, "Is that true?"

"I guess," I said, trying to stand a little taller and look capable of actually hitting someone.

She peered more closely at me. "You being smart with me, son? 'Cause if you are . . ."

"No!" That's all I needed, more trouble. "I mean, it just happened so fast. I didn't realize I was even thinking about hitting him until I saw him there on the ground."

"Hmm." She looked me up and down again and muttered, "Puberty."

I tried not to groan. Beecham was famous for blaming everything that happened at Pierpoint Middle School on puberty. Giggling, punching, fighting, spit wads, back talk: it was all because we were either getting ready to go through puberty or were smack in the middle of it. Everything we did that she didn't like was due to the wicked influences of our hormones, which, according to Beecham, would lead us all down the path to ruin.

"Well, get your testosterone-filled butt up to the office," she told me, "and let the vice principal know what you did. Most likely he'll have a thing or two to say about it." She reached out and grabbed my right hand, making me wince. She examined my knuckles. "You should probably see the nurse, too. She'll get you some ice for the swelling and check for cracked bones."

Funny. I don't ever remember her suggesting that Brandon might have cracked his knuckles when *he* punched *me*.

She dropped my hand and smirked. "They'll be sore for the next week. At least."

I tried to flex my hand, then flinched. Great. When I finally stand up for myself, I get accused of having wimpy knuckles. There is no justice at this school.

Beecham turned back and looked at Brandon as if he were a squashed bug she'd found on her windshield. "You come with me, Blecker. We're going to the nurse's office."

He struggled to his feet. Glaring at me with the promise of revenge in his eyes, he followed Beecham as she marched off. As they went, I could have sworn I heard her say, "Didn't think the little shrimp had it in him."

I was hoping I'd imagined that part.

When my meeting with the vice principal was over, I was so relieved that I forgot all about going to the nurse's office. I made it to fifth period just as the bell rang and slid into my seat next to Joey.

He looked up, surprised to see me back so soon. "Detention?" he whispered.

I shook my head.

"Suspended?" he asked hopefully.

"Nope, nothing. Hobson's just going to call my aunt and uncle and tell them what happened, but that's it."

He stared at me. "They won't even care! You're Mr. Perfect as far as they're concerned."

I snorted. Hardly. In fact, my good grades were one of the few things that Uncle Stephen seemed to actually *like* about me. "That's what a good academic record will do for you. Besides, it *was* self-defense."

By this time, our conversation caught our English teacher's attention. "Mr. Grayson, do you have something you wish to share with the class?"

I slumped down in my seat. "No," I mumbled. That's all I needed, to get in trouble twice today. Joey threw one last envious look my way, and then we settled down to verbs and prepositional phrases, which made my head ache almost as badly as my knuckles.

Except, when I picked up my pen, I found my hand didn't hurt at all anymore and the swelling had disappeared.

3

I was in the kitchen telling Aunt Jane about the incident at school. We were both laughing about the surprised look on Brandon's face when I heard the front door close and Uncle Stephen call out, "Luc!"

"Yeah? I'm in the kitchen with Jane," I called back.

"Come to my study, please. Now."

Jane and I exchanged surprised looks. She shrugged and turned to the sink to start dinner. I'm not allowed in Uncle Stephen's study unless he's there, too, so it's always kind of a big deal when I get called in. He's got a cabinet in there with locks and stuff. I'm not sure what's in it, but once when I was in there and he hadn't closed one of the drawers, I saw a bunch of books. Maybe they have pictures of naked people or something. I never asked. If I was wrong, he'd think I was a pervert. If I was right, well, he'd have just one more reason to be pissed off at me.

Not that he ever comes out and admits he's pissed off at

me, but I can feel it lurking under the surface sometimes. It's as if he's pissed off just because I *exist*.

When I stepped into the study, Uncle Stephen sat behind his desk, tight-lipped and grim. He pointed to a chair, then started talking as soon as I sat down. "I got a call from the vice principal today, Luc. Needless to say, I wasn't happy about it."

I was shocked. Apparently he *was* going to come right out and tell me he was pissed off this time. Part of me was relieved. If he would only explain what he was angry about, I might be able to defend myself. "I was just explaining to Aunt—"

"That's enough!"

My words dribbled to a stop, and I looked at my uncle's face. It was like a mask had been removed. The anger and disgust I saw there made the bottom drop out of my stomach.

"I cannot believe that you hit someone. That you actually struck another person." The softness of Uncle Stephen's voice didn't match the anger in his eyes. "You know how we feel about violence in this house. I've been trying to drum it into you since you were four."

"I know! And it's worked. I've never hit anyone before today."

Uncle Stephen planted his hands on the desk and leaned close. "And now you need to promise me you will never do it again. I need your word."

Promise? Could I promise that? This afternoon the black bubble of anger had swelled up in me and exploded before I'd even realized it was there. I wanted to promise Uncle Stephen, but I wasn't sure I could keep my word. "Well, I think so . . ."

"You *think* so?"

"Well, it *was* Brandon Blecker. I've told you about him. Remember? The awful things he does all the time? Anyway, I don't *intend* to ever hit anyone again, but then I didn't *intend* to hit Brandon today, either. I guess it might depend on what Brandon does in the future."

Uncle Stephen said nothing, he just stared at me, almost as if he were really seeing me for the first time. It was like a black hole had just appeared and swallowed up every single good thing I'd ever done: chores, homework, good grades, honors list. Phht! Gone. Just like that.

"I want your word," he said again.

"And I'd love to give it to you!" Frustrated, I got up from my chair and began pacing around the den. "But it's just . . . I don't know why I hit him in the first place. He kept pushing at me and pushing at me. I asked him to stop. About a hundred times. And he wouldn't. He just laughed and pushed me again. Next thing I know, he's flat on his butt with a bloody nose. How can I give you my word when I couldn't even see this coming?"

Uncle Stephen's face got even grimmer. I felt his eyes on me as I paced. At each turn, I felt his annoyance hitch up a notch, but I couldn't seem to stop myself. I needed to move, as if, somehow, movement would help me figure this thing out.

"Sit!" Uncle Stephen barked. Reacting before I thought about it, I flung myself in the nearest chair, stunned that he'd yelled at me.

Uncle Stephen had always been polite and he treated me well enough, especially in front of other people. But there was also a feeling of emptiness behind it. As if he were just going through the motions because he had to. I mean, if he'd wanted kids, he'd have had them. Getting stuck with an orphaned three-year-old probably wasn't how he'd wanted his life to turn out. But he was my mother's brother. When my parents died in a car crash, he was the only relative I had left. I must have seriously cramped his style.

Or at least, that's what I'd always thought was behind his hidden anger at me. But now, seeing him like this, seeing that anger unmasked, I realized it was personal. He *was* pissed off that I existed. And that I existed under his roof.

"You will not treat this like a joke or some asinine rite of passage. This is a serious offense. You need to understand that this *cannot happen again*. Violence creates more violence, until it never stops." He stood and leaned over his desk. "I will not have you infecting my home with it." He turned away from me to look out the window, as if he couldn't bear the sight of me one second longer.

His home? So much for *our* home. He couldn't have made it more clear that I didn't truly belong here.

Anger spurted through me. This was so unfair. If I was going to get into this much trouble, I should at least have enjoyed hitting the guy.

A quiet little thought slithered through my brain. *You did enjoy it.*

"Go to your room, Luc," Uncle Stephen said without turning around to look at me. "I need to think about your punishment."

"Look, I'm really sorry. I'll call Brandon and—"

"To your room, Luc." His voice cut off my apology, slicing straight through what little friendliness there had ever been between us.

Another gush of anger surged through me, this one hotter and brighter. It made me want to smash my fist into Uncle Stephen's face. My hand curled into a fist at my side.

Terrified by the urge, I stood up. "Fine," I spat out, taking a step backward and knocking the chair to the floor. I turned and ran from the room, leaving the chair where it was.

In the hall, I passed Aunt Jane, who stepped toward me with an apologetic look on her face. I was so mad, and so afraid that I was going to burst into tears of shame and humiliation, that I just shook my head at her and ran to my room, slamming the door behind me. After a moment's hesitation, I locked it.

I threw myself on the bed and glared at the ceiling. Why was Uncle Stephen so angry over this? Why would my hitting someone once make him act as if I'd just joined a gang, shaved my head, pierced my nose, and tattooed my right butt cheek? Even the vice principal hadn't gotten this upset.

I turned to the photograph of my parents that I kept on my bedside table. It was the only picture I had of them. My mom looked up at my dad, and he looked down at her like he was the luckiest man in the world. They were holding a baby between them. Me.

Normally, just looking at that picture cheered me up, but now I felt a painful ache of loneliness. Would they have been furious if I'd punched someone in the nose? Would they have understood? Talked about it with me?

I sighed and got up from the bed and went to the window. It was twilight and the sky was dusky purple with a faint red glow at the horizon where the sun had just gone down.

I didn't just feel restless, I felt caged in. I shoved the window open and let the chilly evening breeze wash against my face. I took a deep breath and felt some of my tension disappear.

While I sat there I suddenly remembered how Uncle Stephen had once explained to me why he rarely got angry. He said it was because anger was closely related to fear. The angrier people got, the more afraid of something they usually were.

As I stared out into the deepening night, I couldn't help but wonder what Uncle Stephen was afraid of.

4

The dream came again that night, leaving me a hollow wreck at 4:30 A.M. This time, I didn't even try to go back to sleep. I wasn't going to risk having that dream twice in one night.

I could already tell it was going to be a lousy day. My nerves were jangled from lack of sleep, I was creeped out that I'd had the same dream again, and I was still ticked off at Uncle Stephen.

No cheerful Mr. Sunshine, me. Still, I made an effort to get off on the right foot. I told Aunt Jane good morning, and she gave me a quick smile over her shoulder as she rinsed out her coffee cup.

I braced myself, waiting for some comment about last night and my new evil self, but all she said was, "Do you want eggs or waffles for breakfast?"

Sausage, I thought. *I want lots and lots of sausage. And bacon.* I shook my head. I never ate that stuff. I was a vegetarian, had been since I was seven and figured out where meat came from. It wasn't because I felt sorry for the animals or anything. It was just too gross to think about, biting into a hunk of something that used to be alive.

"Thanks, Aunt Jane. I think I'll just have some yogurt. It's the Jogathon today, and anything else will just weigh me down." I glanced over at Uncle Stephen, who ignored me as he read the paper at the kitchen table. "And you really don't need to come. Hardly anyone does."

"We'll be there," Uncle Stephen said, making it sound like a threat. "We gave our word, and we keep it."

I rolled my eyes at his thinly veiled dig but got distracted when Aunt Jane put her hand on my shoulder. "We want to be there, Luc. To support you." She glanced meaningfully at Uncle Stephen, who ignored her, too.

"Whatever," I mumbled. I grabbed a container of yogurt and sat down.

Uncle Stephen folded the paper and laid it on the table before looking at me. "I hope you've had time to think about your actions of yesterday. I know I have."

I took a quick spoonful of yogurt so I wouldn't say what I was thinking. Couldn't afford that much more trouble.

Uncle Stephen's mouth tightened up like he'd been sucking on a whole truckload of lemons, and he got a smug, nasty look on his face that was a lot like the one Brandon Blecker got just before he did something really mean. "In order to make sure you understand the seriousness of your offense, Jane and I have decided to cancel your birthday party this weekend."

"What!"

"You heard me. We're canceling your birthday party. I can sell the Sea Hawks tickets or give them away at work today. You can tell Peter, Kyle, and Joey that they aren't going to be able to go to the game. Or sleep over." Stephen stood up. "And be sure to tell them why."

I was speechless as he left the room. Finally, I turned to Aunt Jane, looking for confirmation or explanation or something. She had a very apologetic look on her face. "I'm sorry, Luc. I tried to argue with him, but I'm afraid it was hopeless."

I shook my head in disbelief. "But why?"

Jane shifted her feet and examined the toe of her boot before answering. "He's just worried about you, Luc."

"Yeah, but this is like using a sledgehammer to kill a mosquito! I mean, this is the first time I've ever done anything like this!"

"He just wants to make sure you don't do it again," Aunt Jane said with a worried frown.

"Well, I hate to break it to him, but there are lots of guys in school that get in fights all the time. Joey's already gotten in two fights this year. All his father does is pat him on the back and tell him good work for not letting himself get stomped."

"Yes, but other kids don't—" Jane stopped talking and got busy packing me a lunch.

"Don't what?" I asked.

"It's nothing, really."

"Aunt Jane, tell me! Before I end up hating him." If he could forget nine years of good behavior because of one lousy incident, well, so could I.

Jane looked up, distressed. "Oh, don't hate him, Luc! He's just doing what he thinks is right to make sure you don't end up like—" In exasperation, she stopped and started over again. "You have incidents in your past that are more complicated than other kids'. Stephen feels it's important to make sure those incidents don't scar you in any way." Her eyes were pleading with me to understand, but I didn't. I didn't understand a freaking thing.

"Yeah, but he's acting like one little punch is the first step toward becoming a serial killer."

She dropped the bag of chips she was stuffing into my lunch bag, then bent over to pick it up. When she stood back up, her face was bright red.

A feeling of dread formed in my stomach. "My father wasn't a serial killer, was he?" They'd never said so before, but then, they didn't talk much about my parents. Said it was too painful.

"No! Of course he wasn't. Your father was . . ." Jane paused and blew out a breath. "Your father was a very . . . noble and brave . . . man." She spoke slowly, as if searching for just the right words. "He was a great father to you and loved you very, very much. He would have given his life for you, Luc."

I was speechless. Jane had kept silent for nine years and now she threw me this bone.

"So," she said, breaking the silence, "here's your lunch. You going to be okay?"

I nodded as she handed me the bag.

"I'm sure your friends will understand. It's not like they haven't all been in trouble before. And a lot more often than you."

Exactly! That was my point.

"So, Twinkle Toes, you ready to run in the Jogathon?" Joey asked, bouncing on the balls of his feet as we walked to school.

"Shut up, show-off."

Joey was one of those people who could run like the wind, and he wasn't exactly shy about telling you so. I, on the other hand, was slow. Real slow.

"You know Grimshaw's made it his personal goal in life to get you to run the mile in under eleven minutes."

"Yeah, and thanks ever so much for rubbing it in. What's the matter? Did you have four Pop-Tarts and a Coke for breakfast again?"

He grinned at me. "How'd you guess?"

"Just your typical obnoxious sugar rush, that's all."

He grinned again, reached out, and punched me lightly on the arm. "Come on; I'll race you to school. It'll warm you up." Then he was off, tearing down the street.

I shook my head. Sometimes it was hard to believe we were friends. I stayed behind, walking. There was no way I was going to run any more than I had to.

At eleven o'clock we all stood waiting for Mr. Grimshaw like a flock of bright red sheep. PE clothes are so lame. I think schools do it on purpose as a way to break our spirits and remind us that we're just bodies to be moved from one pen to the next.

Mr. Grimshaw came strolling out of his office with his clipboard in his hand and his whistle and stopwatch around his neck. He once coached college football for two seasons before he got fired, so now he thinks he's exceptionally hot stuff. Mostly he's just a pain.

Our fund-raising event wasn't a true Jogathon. Oh no. That wasn't competitive enough for Coach Grimshaw. It was more of a track-meet-athon. He set up track-and-field events and we got pledges for every one we participated in. And, him being the gung-ho guy that he was, we all had to participate in every one of them.

I glanced up into the stands. There weren't very many parents, but unfortunately, Aunt Jane and Uncle Stephen were there. I'd always appreciated their support before, but now it just felt like Uncle Stephen was going through the motions so he could claim he tried to be a good parent.

Coach Grimshaw blew his whistle twice. We all gathered at the starting line like good little sheep and waited. He loved to draw this moment out. He usually gave an annoying speech about the importance of physical fitness and pushing yourself to do your best, yadda, yadda, yadda.

He blew the whistle one more time, and we all took off. As I passed him, I heard him call out, "Hustle your butt, Grayson. You're going to come in under eleven minutes today or die trying." Apparently nobody in his PE class had ever run as slow as I do, and he took it as a personal affront. Lucky me.

I pushed the old windbag's challenge out of my mind and kept putting one foot in front of the other. Surprisingly, I didn't feel as klutzy as I normally do; my legs seemed to be cooperating for once. And, even more exciting, I didn't immediately drop back to last position. I was still in the middle of the pack. Cool. Maybe Uncle Stephen would be so impressed with my improvement that he'd forget all about being so pissed.

Encouraged by this, I tried to concentrate on what my

body was doing differently so I could repeat it next time. My arms pumped along like well-oiled pistons. They seemed to be in perfect time with my legs, which were striking the track with a rhythm and strength that surprised me. Running felt . . . right somehow. Almost good. Much to my surprise, today I liked running the mile.

Before long I realized I was passing people, kids who'd left me in the dust as far back as I could remember. *Whoosh, whoosh, whoosh* . . . my arms and legs pumped in perfect unison. My lungs filled with oxygen and expanded to meet the challenge. When I realized I was coming in second, right behind Joey, I nearly tripped in shock. Somehow, though, I kept my balance. Some inner competitive urge raised itself inside me. I wanted to beat Joey. Bad. I'd never even been within spitting distance before today, and now I wanted to win more than anything.

I was pretty certain there was no speed left in me—I mean, it was already miraculous, how fast I was going—but I decided to dig a little deeper anyway.

It worked. Steadily, I pulled up right behind Joey, then came alongside him. He glanced over to see who was closing in on him and stumbled—he actually stumbled when he saw it was me.

That was all the edge I needed to cross the finish line first.

I looked up and saw Grimshaw staring at me with his mouth open, his stopwatch lying forgotten in his hand.

"Six-oh-six!" he finally said. "Did you hear me, Grayson? That was six-oh-six. How'd you do that?"

I stood next to Joey, who was bending over with his hands on his knees, panting.

I wasn't even breathing hard. Wasn't tired or anything. The really scary part was, I wanted to run it again.

I looked up into the stands, expecting to see Aunt Jane and Uncle Stephen cheering. Instead, Uncle Stephen's face was white with shock. He looked like he'd just seen a ghost.

I didn't see Joey again until lunch. He was standing in the cafeteria line and made room for me. "Did you bring your lunch?" he asked.

"Yeah. Can't risk eating that cafeteria food." I smiled, but Joey didn't smile back. He looked uncomfortable, like he had something he needed to say and he didn't think I was going to like it. I watched him glance at me sideways, then shuffle his feet for a minute or two before I finally blurted out, "What?"

"You know you only beat me today 'cause I tripped. Right? I mean, I still can't believe you caught up to me. That was totally unbelievable, but the only reason you crossed the finish line first was because I tripped." He stared at me, willing me to believe what he said was true.

He wouldn't even let me have my one moment of glory! Five years of beating the snot out of me, and he couldn't stand that I'd finally beaten him. Would it have killed him to let me have this one win, free and clear?

Seeing the nearly desperate look in his eyes, I realized it might.

"Yeah," I finally said. "I know that's how come I won."

He perked up then, relief making him positively chatty. "Man, you sure put on a good show. Did you see old Grimshaw's face? He was blown away!"

"Well, he wasn't the only one," I said, remembering Uncle Stephen's face.

Joey studied me for a moment, then reached out and punched me on the arm. "Way to go. First, you finally haul off and give Brandon Blecker what he's deserved all year, and now you go and run like a guy for a change. Good job."

Run like a guy? Did that mean he normally thought I ran like a girl? "Gee, thanks, Joey." I reached out and gave him an answering punch on the arm, shocked when he stumbled back and landed on his butt in the cafeteria line, clutching his bicep.

"What was that for?"

"N-nothing. I just gave you a little punch on the arm, like you gave me."

"Yeah, and knocked the spit out of me!" Joey rubbed his arm as he pushed to his feet.

"Hey, I'm really sorry. I didn't mean to." I glanced down at my fist to make sure someone hadn't switched it on me when I wasn't looking.

"Sure, whatever," Joey said, brushing himself off. "Why don't you go run another mile or something," he mumbled.

I stared in shock at Joey. He's only hit me about a thousand times in the five years that we've known each other. I haul off and return the punch *one time,* and he gets his boxers all in a bunch. "What's the matter? Can dish it out but you can't take it. Is that it?"

He set his mouth in a stubborn line and turned his back to me. The line shuffled forward, and I stepped into the cafeteria. The smell of the food nearly knocked me back two steps. I looked over at Joey, to see if he'd noticed it, but he still wasn't looking at me. Slowly, I took another breath, and my lungs filled with something that reeked of vomit, body odor, and tomato sauce. It was so rank there was no way I could set foot into that room without being sick. Trying not to gag, I stepped out of line and went out to the concrete bleachers by the amphitheater.

I sat down and began munching on my cheese sandwich, trying not to feel like a total loser for eating by myself. I pretended to be fascinated by a group of squirrels that were running up and down the tree trunks collecting leftover lunch scraps.

It wasn't until I was halfway through my sandwich that I found myself wondering what squirrels tasted like. As I wondered, I could almost feel their fur on my tongue, feel the pulsing plumpness of their little bodies in my mouth.

Shuddering, I stuffed my sandwich into my lunch bag. I'd suddenly lost my appetite.

5

By the time I got home from school, I was sicker than a dog. At first, I thought it was from running so hard. Then I thought maybe it was the cafeteria, but that didn't make sense. The cafeteria stank all the time; that was nothing new.

Feeling too miserable to watch TV, I crawled into bed and got under the covers. I lay there, shivering and feeling like my insides were trying to crawl out through my skin.

I think I dozed, because the next thing I knew, I heard a loud click, then the sound of the front door swinging open. Funny, I'd never *heard* the door open before. Then, right away, I knew it was Aunt Jane. Not because she always got home first. She doesn't. But I could *smell* her. I mean, she doesn't stink or anything. But I could smell her particular smell, the perfume she always wore, the fabric softener she used when she did the laundry, all topped off with the faint aroma of the café mocha she must have drunk this afternoon.

"Luc?" she called out.

"I'm in my room," I called back.

"Are you feeling any better? I'm sorry I couldn't get off work when you called." When she appeared in the doorway, my senses were swamped with Jane smells. She'd had chicken Caesar salad for lunch, and at some point during the day she stepped in dog poop because I caught a strong whiff of that. She'd driven through roadwork on the way home because the smell of asphalt clung to her clothes. And skin. I could smell Aunt Jane's skin. How sick is that?

"Still feeling lousy, huh?" she asked, sympathy filling her voice.

"Yeah," I answered.

"Are you sure you're not just feeling blue over your canceled birthday? I'd understand if you were." She walked over and placed her cool hand on my forehead. "Well, you *are* a little feverish. I'll take your temperature in a bit. Just stay tucked up in bed, and I'll go start dinner."

I nodded, not wanting to talk unless I had to.

As I lay in bed, I heard Jane getting out pots and pans to make dinner. They rattled and banged so loudly, it made my ears ache. I closed my eyes and pulled my pillow over my head to block out the noise. Before long, the smell of salmon cooking crept into my room. It was so strong, I almost couldn't bear it. But at the same time, it made me so hungry, I wanted to run in there and eat the stuff raw.

My stomach gurgled and heaved, and I pulled the wastebasket closer to the bed.

After Stephen and Jane had dinner, I shuffled out into the living room for a change of scenery. Just that little bit of activity made me feel weak and shaky. I hated being sick like this.

One minute I was so cold, I needed to pile on six blankets. Then I got so hot I threw them all off, stripped out of my sweatpants, and lay there in my boxers, trying to cool off. I was as weak as a baby bird, yet restless, like I wanted to run the mile again. Maybe twice. My fingertips were numb, but my cheeks were burning. My skin itched and twitched.

"I still think I should call the doctor." Jane stood at the foot of the couch, looking down at me with worried eyes.

"He's fine, Jane," Uncle Stephen called from his study.

"I don't know. He's really pale and his eyes look feverish to me. I really think he needs to see the doctor."

"Nonsense. He's just made himself sick showing off at the Jogathon today. Or maybe guilt is rearing its ugly head."

It was a good thing I was so sick because if not, I would have been *so* off this couch and slamming my fist into Stephen's face. I'd had enough of his cheap shots.

Ever since Stephen had come home from work, he'd refused to be in the same room with me. He wasn't being obvious about it, but I'd noticed just the same. And he wouldn't look at me. His eyes just kind of slipped over me, like I didn't exist. It made me feel like such a lowlife. Which pissed me off because all I'd done was punch someone *once* and win the Jogathon for a change. Sheesh. The way he was acting, you'd think I'd turned into a monster or something.

Jane reached down and patted me on the ankle. "Okay. No doctor for now. But the good news is no school tomorrow, either. And try to stop scratching."

"It's the weekend," I reminded her. "There's no school tomorrow anyway."

"Shouldn't be around others till you get your behavior under control anyway," Uncle Stephen muttered from the doorway. Once again, I could feel little waves of anger rolling off him. And there was that whiff of something else. Fear. Since when did fear have a smell, anyway?

"I'm going to get you some soup." Aunt Jane had been trying to stuff me full of broth and soda crackers all evening. What I was really dying for was a nice juicy steak, hold the baked potato. Only problem was, I didn't think I could choke it down. Well, that and the fact that I was a vegetarian. But thinking about it sure got my mouth watering. This was some weird flu!

When Aunt Jane stepped into the hallway, she began to argue with Uncle Stephen in a low, angry voice. She was pleading with him to call the doctor or someone else, someone whose name I didn't catch. But Uncle Stephen barked at her to be quiet.

He was my legal guardian. He was supposed to see that I got proper medical treatment. Maybe I could sue him for reckless endangerment. That's it. As soon as I could take a step outside this condo, I was suing his ears off.

Just as I was getting to the really good part of my fantasy, where Uncle Stephen gets down on his knees in front of the entire courtroom and begs my forgiveness, someone knocked on the door. The arguing in the hallway stopped, and my aunt and uncle came out into the living room.

Still not looking at me, Uncle Stephen went to the door and opened it, then hissed. Hissed!

And then I got a whiff of whoever stood on the other side of the door. He smelled of wind, and rain, and the night, of pine trees, and secret places. Of danger, and something else—home.

The stranger ignored Uncle Stephen's protests and

pushed right past him into the room. Jane clamped her hand over her mouth and stared as if the living dead had just appeared in her front room. The stranger glanced briefly at her and nodded courteously, almost a bow. She finally took her hand from her mouth. "Ranger! He-hello." Her face held no fear like Stephen's. More like awe and fascination, and maybe even relief.

The man was tall and lean and stood with an unnatural stillness. Droplets of rain ran off his black trench coat onto the rug beneath his feet. His dark hair was pulled back into a ponytail, his face hard-edged and sharp. But it was his eyes that stood out the most. They were a rich, glowing gold. I'd never seen eyes that color.

"Dad?" The word escaped before I could stop it. He looked exactly like the picture of my father I had in my bedroom . . . well, except for the trench coat and the ponytail and the eyes. I knew it couldn't really be my father. He'd been dead for nine years. But something about this man seemed familiar to me. As if somewhere deep inside my bones, I knew him.

The stranger turned to glare at Uncle Stephen. "You've told him nothing about me?"

To his credit, Uncle Stephen held his ground, even though he flinched. Me? I would have run screaming if that man had looked at me like that. "Nothing," he spat out. "Not one word."

"And what of his parents? What have you told him about them?"

At the question, a heavy silence filled the room, and it felt as if everything I thought was real and true hung in the balance.

"The truth," Uncle Stephen said at last. "That they died in a car crash."

With a look of disgust, the stranger turned back to me. When our eyes met, I sensed an energy from him. It snaked across the room like a fast-drifting fog. No, not fog. It was warm, much warmer than that. Like a wisp of smoke. When it reached me, it hovered a minute, as if testing the air right above my body. I knew the second it touched me. The energy spread across my skin in a warm, tingling rush, causing every single hair on my body to stand up. I'd been hot all day, feverish. But this warmth was different. The heat had a healing feel to it. For the first time today, something inside my gut untwisted and I was able to take a full breath.

I knew in that moment that this man was no stranger. Whoever he was—and I still didn't have a clue—he was the one person in the room who just might be able to save me. From what, I wasn't sure, but I suddenly felt as if I desperately needed to be saved.

With his eyes still on me, he spoke to Uncle Stephen. "I've come to take Luc home."

Uncle Stephen glanced at me, his eyes uncertain. "I'm his guardian. I'm the one the courts granted custody to. Me. Not you."

The man turned to my uncle and stared at him with contempt. "Only because you lied under oath."

Stephen paled. "Everything I said was true. You weren't fit to keep him then, and you're not fit to keep him now. I'm the only one who can keep him safe."

Safe from what? I wanted to scream.

The man ignored Uncle Stephen's words and pushed farther into the room. "He isn't safe here. He will never be safe here. Just look at him!"

Uncle Stephen turned and looked at me, and I didn't like what I saw in his face. It was hard and mean. With a jolt, I realized it was hate. But why should he hate me? Because I'd hit somebody?

Then realization smacked me right between the eyes. The punching had only been an excuse. An excuse to let out his true feelings for me.

"The boy is coming with me, Stephen. It is his heritage. He must shift, and he must shift soon. And with others there to guide him."

At those words, Uncle Stephen took two steps back. "He is not like you," he said, his voice uneasy, almost as if he was trying to convince himself. "He's not like you, not like his father! Do you hear me? I raised him away from all of you so he could grow up free of your influence. I gave him a chance at a normal life and tried to keep him from turning into an abomination."

The stranger's jaw tightened. "At thirteen, the courts will let him have some say in the matter."

As far as I could tell, there was no choice. If the stranger offered a way to escape, I was taking it.

Aunt Jane took a step forward and placed her hand on Stephen's arm. "Maybe it would be for the best."

He shrugged her off.

In two easy strides that ate up the small room, Ranger came to stand in front of me. He crouched down and studied me as if he were counting my molecules. "Feeling badly, are you?"

Those eyes of his called the truth from me, even if I'd

wanted to lie, which I didn't. I nodded. Even all the drama unfolding before me couldn't keep me from shivering, miserable and frightened.

Ranger turned around, his face a study in controlled fury. "Look at him, Stephen. Look how sick he is. He needs help."

"Not your kind of help."

"He needs exactly my kind of help." Ranger turned back to me. "Are you afraid?"

I nodded.

"Of course he's terrified," Stephen interjected. "Who wouldn't be with a madman bursting into his home?"

Ranger studied me. "Is that why you're afraid?"

I shook my head. That wasn't what scared me. What scared me was the feeling that something terrible was going to happen. And soon.

"Do you wish to stay here or come with me?" the stranger asked.

I turned from his warm, understanding eyes to Uncle Stephen's cold, distant ones. There was no reason for Uncle Stephen to treat me like this. I hadn't done anything to deserve it. So forget him. He'd see he couldn't treat me that way and get away with it. I turned back to Ranger. "I'll go with you."

The area around Uncle Stephen's mouth turned white. "If that's the way you feel, then maybe you should go with him. Maybe that would be best." His voice was low and flat.

Ranger reached down and picked me up, holding me in his arms like I was an infant. I'm five-two and weigh a hundred pounds, but he didn't even grunt when he picked me up. He looked down at me, his eyes gentle. "Hang on just a little longer, Luc."

As I hung there waiting for something to happen next, I felt like I should say something, at least to Aunt Jane. But what? In the end I said nothing, but looked silently at Aunt Jane, pleading with her to understand. I think she did.

Ranger turned toward the door, and clutched in the stranger's arms and feeling like death warmed over, I stepped out of my old life and into my new one.

Or would have, if I'd been able to walk.

6

Ranger carried me down the hallway and out the front door of the building. It was raining, but to my surprise, being outside in the cold, wet night air made me feel better. I lifted my face up to the rain and felt it wash away the trembling a little bit.

As if reading my thoughts, Ranger asked, "Feeling better?"

"Yeah," I answered, surprised. "I am."

Ranger allowed himself a tiny smile as he walked to his car. It was a big black SUV with mud splattered halfway up the body. He set me down and unlocked the passenger door, holding it for me while I climbed in. I was still trembling and shivering, but that didn't seem nearly as important as the thousands of questions that were pounding in my head.

Ranger got into the car. I started to ask him a question, but he took my chin in his fingers and turned it first to the left, then to the right. Using his thumb, he pushed back my lips and had a quick look at my teeth. When he was finished, he said, "Hands."

Puzzled, I held them up, and he studied the palms before turning them over and checking the backs. He nodded. "Good." Then he turned to start the engine.

Okay. So that was a little weird. I cleared my throat and tried again. "So, you knew my father?"

He tensed for a moment, then turned to face me. "Yes, I knew your father. He was my brother. My older brother."

My mouth dropped open in shock. "So you're my uncle."

"Yes. I'm your uncle."

Something inside me clicked, and I felt like I was falling from a great distance, dizzy and unbalanced and unable to catch myself. "B-but they told me . . . there was no one else. That Stephen was my only family left."

"They lied." Ranger rubbed a hand over his face. "Look, it's a long story, but the important thing is this: I am your uncle and the one your parents appointed as your guardian. I'm who they wanted you to be with if something ever happened to them. Hopefully, that will make you feel better about coming with me."

Maybe that explained why I felt so comfortable with him. Why I was willing to leave everything I knew and follow him to who knew where. Maybe some part of me had recognized him. Even so, I couldn't help but wonder. "What took you so long?" I asked. "I mean, to find me. Claim me. Whatever."

"Like I said. It's a long story, and you heard some of it in there. Stephen didn't like your father, and he didn't like me. He effectively blocked my guardianship."

But I barely heard the rest of his explanation as my mind latched on to his words. Uncle Stephen hadn't liked my father. He'd sounded like he hated him, back in the condo.

That would explain so much. "Is that why Uncle Stephen hates me?" I blurted out.

Ranger frowned. "Does he hate you, Luc?"

I looked away from his sympathetic gaze. "Yeah. It seems like it. Especially lately."

"Then that is most likely why." Ranger turned his eyes to the road and pulled out into traffic. "I know you have many questions, but it would be better if they could wait. Plus you should try and get some sleep. You'll feel better after a nap."

Maybe. But the main reason I kept quiet was that he'd given me enough to think about already. Besides, he wasn't the kind of person you argued with.

Bright lights shining against my eyelids woke me up. That and the sense that the car wasn't moving anymore. I opened my eyes and sat up quickly—too quickly. My head went all woozy, and I had a horrible, blank moment when I couldn't remember where I was or why.

Then it all came flooding back. Stephen. Ranger. Piling into a big mud-splattered SUV.

I worked the kinks out of my neck, then turned to look over at the driver's side. Ranger sat patiently, watching me with those see-all, know-all eyes of his. "You awake?"

"Yeah," I said, rubbing my eyes.

"Lost Pines is the last town for a while. Do you feel like eating something? Making a bathroom stop?" he asked.

I started to tell him that I felt too sick to eat anything, but my stomach let out a huge rumble just then. "Uh, yeah, guess I *am* hungry."

He smiled. "Then let's get you something to eat."

We got out of the car, and I felt the crunch of gravel

under my feet. The smell of pine and the cold sharp smell of the mountains helped clear the sleep from my brain. Ranger led me to a small log cabin–style building with a sign that said LOST PINES CAFÉ.

As we reached the door, another car turned into the parking lot behind us. Ranger stiffened, then turned to watch the black sedan pull into a parking space in the farthest corner.

"What?" I asked, not surprised to find myself whispering.

He looked from the car back to me. "Nothing." Without further explanation, he opened the door to the café and we walked in.

All the talking stopped, and twenty pairs of eyes turned to look at us. The overwhelming smell of too many people in too small a space hit me just before the rush of energy. Prickles ran along the back of my neck. I glanced at Ranger, but he seemed unaffected. I looked back at the crowd. One ogre-size man with crazy-looking blue eyes wouldn't stop looking at me. He was so aggressive about it that it began to really bug me. I don't know why he was staring like that, but right then and there I swore I wouldn't look away first.

The staring match stretched out, like a giant rubber band between the two of us. It kept getting tighter and tighter until finally Ranger grabbed my arm and pulled me toward a table. Reluctant to go, I kept my eyes on Ogre Bill and asked Ranger under my breath, "What's he looking at?"

With a screech of chair legs against the rough wooden floor, the man stood. He looked like he was going to barrel across the room after me. My heart thudded so loudly, I was sure everyone in the room could hear it, but I still refused to look away.

Ranger snarled and grabbed me by the scruff of the neck, shaking me slightly before hauling me over to a table. He shoved me into a seat while he stared back at Ogre Bill. Finally, the other man nodded, and the tension in the room went down a notch or two.

Slowly, Ranger looked at each of the other diners, one by one, smack in the eye, until they all looked away.

Handy trick. I wouldn't mind learning how to do that.

I leaned forward so I could speak softly. "What was all that about?"

Much to my relief, he didn't play dumb and say, "All what?"

"We are strangers in their territory. They are weighing us, trying to get the feel of our intentions."

Yeah, right. Made perfect sense to me. Not.

A waitress came to our table. Her eyes were all over Ranger like he was a hot-fudge sundae and she was starving to death. "What'll you two have?"

Ranger motioned for me to answer first. "I'll have the biggest cheeseburger you've got. With bacon," I said, surprised to find my appetite was back. And for meat. "Rare," I added, without even thinking.

"Fries or coleslaw with that?"

That's one of the stupidest questions on the face of the planet. Who ever picks coleslaw to go with anything? "Fries. And a chocolate milk shake."

She turned to Ranger again, her eyes glowing. "And you."

He shook his head. "Nothing for me. Just water." She paused, looking as if she wanted to say more, but didn't.

When she'd left, I asked him, "Aren't you hungry?"

"No," was his reply. "I had a big meal yesterday."

Hel-lo? Everybody ate some kind of big meal yesterday; that doesn't mean they aren't hungry today.

The waitress brought us our drinks. As I took a big sip of my chocolate milk shake, I realized that the farther away we got from the city, the better I felt. The chills were gone, and so was the achy trembling. Encouraged, I decided I was up for some more questions. I started with the most painful one. "Why did Stephen call my father an abomination?"

Ranger's jaw clenched, then he forced himself to relax. "Because some people are afraid of what they cannot understand."

"Oh," I said in a very small voice. "What did Uncle Stephen do to keep you from taking custody of me earlier?"

Ranger's nostrils flared and his mouth flattened. "He lied under oath in the custody courts, accused me of being something I'm not, and have never been. He had your parents declared unfit to make the decision of whom to entrust you with."

The anger I felt for Stephen ramped up, rolling along at a slow boil just below the surface. How could I go from caring about someone to practically hating him in less than a week? It made my head spin. "Why now?" I asked. "I mean, why did you come for me tonight?"

"Because your thirteenth birthday is in two days. I needed to find you before then."

"Why?"

"Because the thirteenth birthday is when a person passes out of childhood and into something else."

I nodded. Maybe all this crap *did* have to do with puberty.

Just then the waitress placed my burger in front of me. I

forgot all my questions as the smell of perfectly charred beef covered with melting cheese swamped my senses.

Ranger smiled, as if reading my mind. "Eat," he invited.

And eat I did. I wolfed down that food like there was no tomorrow. I was so focused on consuming that burger that I decided all the other questions could wait.

It took about three minutes for me to finish my dinner, I was that hungry. As I slurped up the last bits of my milk shake, I could sense Ranger getting restless.

"Are you done?" he asked.

I nodded, and he took some bills from his pocket and tossed them onto the table. "Then let's go."

I followed him out of the café, excruciatingly aware of all the eyes boring into our backs as we made our way. I scanned the crowd and found Ogre Bill looking at me again. I narrowed my eyes at him, then felt Ranger grab the scruff of my neck and pull me forward.

"Are you trying to get into a fight tonight?" He sounded both exasperated and amused.

"No! I just don't like him staring at me like that."

With his hand still on my neck, we stepped outside. I smelled the clean scent of the giant trees around us. I could almost feel the sap flowing through their branches. I glanced up, shocked by how bright and close the stars seemed. You'd swear you could reach up and pluck one from the sky.

We took two steps toward the car, then Ranger stopped, his eyes going to the far corner of the lot. The black sedan was still there.

With his hand still on my neck, he switched directions and propelled me toward a motel next to the café. "We'll stay here tonight, then get on the road at first light."

"Is something wrong?" I asked, looking back at the car.

"No." The word fell between us like a small pebble, then rolled away into the night.

Not surprisingly, the motel had plenty of cabins available. When Ranger opened the door to Cabin Six, the first thing that struck me was the musty smell. Ranger must have noticed it, too, because he immediately went around and opened all the windows. Then he turned to me. "You need to get to sleep. I'll want to leave by dawn."

I went and used the bathroom, then splashed some water on my face. Deciding that wasn't enough, I took a quick hot shower.

I came out and found the bed turned down, all cozy and welcoming like. Ranger was sitting in the chair next to the open window, staring out into the night.

I climbed into bed and pulled up the covers, trying to get comfortable, but I had one last question.

"You know . . ." I laughed nervously. "I don't know what to call you. Uncle? Ranger? What?"

He smiled in the moonlight. "Ranger is fine. That's what everyone calls me."

I could live with that. I didn't think I could call him uncle yet. Besides, that word wasn't my favorite since Uncle Stephen's disloyalty. I started to open my mouth to ask another question, but Ranger's quiet voice interrupted. "Sleep, Luc. We can talk later."

I wondered if he was a hypnotist, because all he had to do was look at me and I felt like I *had* to do whatever he asked. I snuggled down under the covers, my body very happy to be lying down flat, not all wadded up in the car. "'Night, then."

"Good night," he said from his chair. I was tempted to ask if he planned on sleeping, but I didn't.

It only took a few minutes to reach that delicious state of almost sleep, where you're so relaxed it's as if you've separated from your body, but you're still conscious enough to realize you're not asleep. Since my eyes were closed, I felt rather than saw Ranger get up from his chair. I expected to hear the bedsprings on the other bed sag as he lay down, but I didn't. Instead, I heard the squeak of a rusty hinge, felt a cold gush of air, and then heard the soft click as the door closed.

My eyes popped open. Ranger was gone. I lay there a minute trying to decide what to do. He wouldn't leave me. That didn't make any sense. Why would he drive all the way to Seattle to get me, then abandon me in some lumberjack village? He was probably just going for a walk or something, needed some fresh air.

As soon as my mind landed on that thought, I knew it was true. He seemed restless whenever he was inside. Maybe the musty smell of the cabin bothered him even more than it bothered me. Curious, I threw off the covers and got out of bed, my toes curling away from the cold floor. I went over to the chair Ranger had sat in. His scent still clung to it. I couldn't wait to get over being sick. I hated being so aware of the way everything smelled. It made the inside of my nose hurt.

I peered out the window to the gravel parking lot. I saw Ranger's car, but no sign of him. My gaze drifted to the woods surrounding the motel. The trees were enormous. Pale moonlight fell down on their branches, casting long black and gray shadows. I leaped back from the window when I saw two yellow eyes staring at me from one of the darker shadows. Heart hammering in my throat, I rubbed the fog of my breath off the window with my sleeve and forced myself to look again.

A great black dog, the biggest I'd ever seen, stood beneath the trees staring right at me. He was big and powerful, with massive shoulders and long, spindly legs. He seemed almost tall enough to stand eyeball to eyeball with me. Not that I wanted to be anywhere near that close.

Just then, the clouds shifted and he stood clearly visible in the moonlight. I gasped.

That was no dog. That was a wolf.

Suddenly I was hugely grateful for the thick cabin wall and the parking lot that separated us.

As if sensing my fear, the wolf tilted his head to the sky and howled: a long, eerie sound that filled the night. It sent shivers down my back and filled me with a sense of wonder. I felt a tug in my own throat, an almost overwhelming urge to answer that cry with one of my own.

Before I did anything that stupid, the wolf turned and moved deeper into the forest. The last I saw of him was his shadowy black shape loping under the pale moonlight.

7

When I opened my eyes the next morning, Ranger was in the same armchair he'd been in last night. And he was still watching me. "Good morning, Luc," he said.

I mumbled, "Good morning," and then it hit me. I hadn't had the dream! Not once during the night had I dreamed of the things that had been haunting me. I'd slept deeply, dreaming of running through clean forests with the moon at my side.

"'Morning, Ranger," I said again, suddenly cheerful.

"I've got breakfast right here." He nodded to a white bag on the table next to him. "If you don't mind, I'd rather you eat in the car so we can get on the road as soon as possible."

"Sure. No problem." I jumped out of bed. I mean, I really jumped out of bed. Gone were the fever, the chills, the trembling, everything. For the first time in about three days, my skin acted like it was happy to stay right where it was. Sweet! I looked at Ranger in wonder. "You were right! I'm all better. And I didn't even have the dream."

"What dream?" Ranger asked, immediately curious.

"Never mind. It's just some stupid nightmare I've been having. But I'm cured. That's the important thing."

Ranger looked like he wanted to ask more about my dream. I kept right on talking so he wouldn't. "Do you know why I feel better? You told me last night to hang on a little longer. Did you know I would get better soon?"

"I knew that once I got you away from Stephen and out in the forest, closer to home, you'd begin to feel better."

"Is it the fresh mountain air?" I asked, stepping into my shoes.

He smiled. "In part. It's also the nearness of wild things and the closeness of your ancestors' spirits. And I am loaning you a little bit of my power as well."

That stopped me cold. "Power. You're lending me power. Like what? Electrical or natural gas?" I had been trying for a joke, but it fell flat.

He quirked his eyebrow at me. "Not that kind of power. My . . . personal power, if you will. My own body's energy."

I rolled my eyes. "Are you a New Ager? Because if so, I gotta warn you right now that I'm not too big on that stuff." I'd had my fill of it when Aunt Jane went through her New Age phase a few years back.

Ranger stared at me with those patient golden eyes, and I immediately felt guilty for making fun of him. I mean, he *had* made me feel better, whatever he'd done.

"You know what I'm talking about, Luc. You felt it when I first walked into Stephen's house. It's how you knew I was safe."

He had me there. I *had* felt his power, or something, snake across the room.

Ranger stood up. "Come here."

I took a few cautious steps forward.

"Stop. Now close your eyes and use your other senses. Can you feel my power?"

I concentrated and did sense something. A slight buzzing sensation, as if his skin were humming. But silently. "Yeah. I do."

"Now step closer."

I took two steps forward, and caught my breath as the sensation amped up, zooming up and down my skin. I stepped back, shook my head to clear it. I felt refreshed and energized. "Wow."

"Yeah," Ranger said, smiling. "Wow. Now come on. Let's hit the road."

I followed him outside, then stopped. Everything—the trees, the mist, the cabins, the gravel—looked as if it had been painted with a giant brush dipped in golden pink.

Ranger stepped off the porch and went to the car. I followed, reluctant to leave. I glanced over at the clearing where the wolf had been last night.

"What?" Ranger asked. Then he sniffed. He looked at me strangely. "What do you have in your pockets?"

Frowning, I patted my pockets and felt my cell phone. I pulled it out. "Oh, this?"

Ranger snatched the phone out of my hand, threw it on the ground, and crushed it with the heel of his boot. Then he carried it over to the motel's Dumpster and tossed it in.

I gaped in disbelief. "Hey! That was an expensive gift! I might need it out here."

"There's no signal where we're going," he said, then turned and strode toward the car.

Maybe not, but he didn't have to destroy it, did he? I followed him to the car and got in. As Ranger pulled onto the open highway, I turned back and looked in the café parking lot to see if the black sedan was still there. It wasn't.

He nudged me on the shoulder. When I turned around, he handed me a white bag. From the smell, I knew exactly what was in there. Doughnuts. My favorite breakfast. "Thanks!"

Cell phone forgotten, I bit into the chocolate doughnut. Nothing had ever tasted so good.

I licked the last of the glaze crumbs from my fingers and said, "I saw a wolf last night."

Ranger glanced at me sharply, and I mentally thumped myself on the head for being such a motormouth. "Did you?" he asked.

I shrugged. "Yeah." Too late to pull back now. "He was right outside the ring of cabins, in the shadows of the trees. It was right after you left to go for your walk."

"Were you afraid?"

I thought for a minute. "No, not afraid. More like . . . hypnotized." Embarrassed at the word, I kept talking. "He . . . it . . . stared right at me, as if it were trying to read my mind or something. It was really . . . intense. So," I said, changing the subject, "where are you taking me?"

"The community where I live. And where you shall live also, from now on."

"A community? Is that like a town, or a city or something?"

"More like a small village."

Village, I thought. Such an old-fashioned word. "So what's it like?"

"It's small, deep in the woods."

"So what kind of job do you have, living so far out in the boondocks?"

"I am Fenriki. A . . . diplomatic agent, is probably the best way to describe it."

"What country do you work with?"

Ranger smiled. "Here in the United States."

"Oh. Don't diplomats usually work in foreign countries or something?"

"Not always. Not with the kind of diplomatic work I do."

"What, exactly, do you do?"

"Keep relations smooth between our village and the surrounding population. Other villages like ours, too."

That was odd. I'd never heard of cities, let alone small villages in the middle of nowhere, having a diplomat to keep relations running smoothly. Asking Ranger questions was pointless. All I got back were answers that led to more questions. Frustrating. I gave up and stared out the window, watching the highway whiz by, mesmerized by the white lines flashing like a strobe light. As I watched, I imagined myself running alongside the car, faster and faster, until I, too, flashed past the concrete so quickly I was nothing but a blur.

As we drew closer to the mountains, all the questions that had crowded my mind when Ranger first arrived slowly slipped away. Everything about me felt smooth. Connected. There were no bumps or rough spots anywhere. I was filled with a sense of safety and wholeness that I had never experienced before. Which seems strange when you realize what a city kid I am. The few times I'd been camping, I hadn't been impressed. No TV, no computer, no CDs, just lots of air, mountains, trees, and dirt. But today, it seemed perfect.

I must have hypnotized myself into some kind of a trance or something because the next thing I knew we had pulled off the highway onto a dirt road that led even farther into the trees. We bumped and shuddered along, the road much too jarring to either sleep or talk. The reason Ranger drove an SUV was painfully clear to me. And my butt.

After a while we turned onto a smaller dirt road that looked more like a deer track. We bounced along that until I thought about begging to get out of the car and run along-side. It wouldn't be any slower, and it felt like my teeth were going to come loose. Just as I opened my mouth, I caught sight of a shadow flashing in the trees alongside of us.

Squinting, I looked more carefully. There was some-thing . . . something big . . . running just beyond the trees that lined the road. I finally caught the rhythm and antici-pated where the next break in the trees would be. There! It flashed out from behind the shadows; a long leggy body with huge shoulders and a large, tapered head.

It was another wolf! Running alongside our car.

I turned to Ranger in disbelief. "There's a wolf . . ."

Ranger smiled. "I know."

"But . . ."

"There are a lot of wolves around here, Luc."

I turned back to the window, disappointed when the wolf was no longer in sight. A howl rose up from the trees where the wolf had been, making me shiver. I heard Ranger whisper under his breath, "And greetings to you, too, Nuri."

Before I could ask him to explain what he'd meant by that, we turned at one more bend in the road and pulled up before a small clearing. The town was nothing but a few wooden buildings nestled among a cluster of giant pine trees. It reminded me of one of those pioneer towns you see in old Western movies on TV sometimes. Only this was set against a rich, green forest, not some dusty old frontier. A sinking feeling filled my chest. This couldn't be—

"Welcome home," Ranger said, then brought the car to a stop.

8

There were more than a dozen people gathered in front of the SUV. They were rustic-looking, with flannel shirts and funny-looking pants that had drawstrings instead of zippers. They wore moccasins or old leather boots, but no sneakers or recognizable Nike logo or anything. Both the women and the men had long hair. It kind of reminded me of Early Hippie meets Lumberjack City. Oh boy. This should be fun. I swallowed, then got out of the car.

A tall man stepped forward. He was taller than Ranger, and just as strong-looking. His brown hair went down to his shoulders and was streaked with gray. His eyes were a golden green. He glanced briefly at me, then turned to Ranger.

I watched in disbelief as Ranger, Mr. Stare-You-Down-Until-You-Grovel, averted his gaze and bowed his head slightly. "I have returned, Ulric. I bring Kennet's son and ask that he be given the pack's protection and be allowed to take his proper place."

I couldn't have been more surprised if Ranger had opened his mouth and toads had jumped out. And what did he mean, protection?

The older man threw his arms around Ranger, and they gave each other a big bear hug. The older man—Ranger had called him Ulric—still hadn't given me more than a glance, and he hadn't answered Ranger's plea for my acceptance. He lowered his voice. "Do you think you were followed?"

Ranger nodded and answered so quietly that I couldn't hear. I was so intent on listening that the brown shadow that streaked out from behind the trees didn't fully register.

Until it hit me.

Pain, hot and raw, shot up my arm. There was a heavy thud against my chest, then all the air whooshed out of my lungs as I slammed into the ground. Before I could make sense of anything, I was flat on my back staring up at a snarling wolf.

Musk and damp fur filled my senses. Sharp white teeth were inches from my throat, and the worst dog breath imaginable huffed in my face.

Terrified, I looked into a pair of liquid brown eyes that held equal parts intelligence and threat. Too petrified to even breathe, I could only wonder where Ranger was now that I really needed him.

There was a deep, low growl, then I felt a sharp, prickly rush of power, followed by the enormous weight on my chest disappearing, along with the vicious teeth that seemed to have my name all over them.

Once free, I scrambled back a few feet on all fours until my arms collapsed, rubbery with fear. A big, brown-and-gray wolf had pinned a smaller one on the ground. His teeth were buried in the smaller wolf's throat. The big wolf shook his head and snarled through the wad of fur he held in his mouth.

I jumped slightly when Ranger squatted down beside me. "Are you okay?" His hands were gentle as they felt my neck for any serious wounds.

"I'm okay. Just terrified." I pulled my gaze away from the two wolves and looked at Ranger. "Why did he attack me? Does that happen often around here? Because I'm not sure I want to live someplace with wild animals roaming around." Fear had me babbling like an idiot.

"No, they never attack. Believe it or not, that was a greeting. And Nuri is being punished for it."

Nuri. That was the name Ranger had mentioned in the car. I turned back to the wolves, but they were gone. The man who'd greeted Ranger was towering over a kid about my age. The kid sat huddled on the ground, his eyes cast down, every fiber of his being limp and unresisting. Ulric was livid, I could tell.

"How dare you! It is my place to greet any newcomers to the pack. Not yours."

Still not looking at the older man, the kid answered, "I was just trying to be friendly. You were busy talking to Ranger, and he was standing there all alone, so I thought it was okay."

Faster than my eye could follow, the older man grabbed the boy's neck and forced him to the ground again. "I was still talking with my Fenriki to see how their journey had gone," he growled. "What will it take for Teague to pound some learning into that thick head of yours?" Ulric shoved the boy's head back, but lightly, then stood up and turned to us. He reached out and offered me his hand. "Are you all right?"

Since I'd just seen him take that kid to the ground, I wasn't about to risk offending him. I took his hand and let him pull me to my feet. "Yeah, I'm okay. Just a little shaken up."

The man's nostrils flared. "You're bleeding." He quickly found the scratch on my arm and examined it with surprisingly gentle fingers. "It's shallow. It should heal quickly."

I was less worried about my wound than I was about the wolves. I looked around the clearing. "So where did the wolves go?"

The older man looked over at Ranger and raised his eyebrows.

Ranger shook his head slightly. "He doesn't know."

The other man bit back a sound of disgust. He turned back to me, grabbed my shoulders, and stared deeply into my eyes. "I, Ulric of the Golwyg Pack, welcome you, Luc Grayson, son of Kennet, into our pack." Then he pulled me toward him and kissed my right cheek then my left.

At those words, the crowd began to murmur. I'd completely forgotten about them. They surged forward, words of greeting and welcome on their lips. I found myself thumped on the shoulder and heartily patted on the back. My hand was shaken and my cheeks pinched.

Ulric's voice boomed across the clearing. "There will be a formal greeting ceremony at dinner tonight. Until then, go about your business and let this young pup get settled."

Still murmuring happy sounds, the crowd moved away,

going back to whatever they were doing when we'd first arrived.

Finally, I found myself face-to-face with Ranger. He, too, gave me a kiss on each cheek. "Welcome home, Luc."

"Home? Pack? What is everyone talking about?"

At my puzzled look, Ranger spoke. "Have you not guessed?"

Guessed what? Slowly little bits and pieces were starting to click into place in my mind, but they didn't make any sense, challenged everything I knew about reality.

"You, like your father before you, are a lycanthrope. And we are the pack to which you belong."

"A lycanthrope?" I stammered stupidly.

"Yes, Luc. Or what some would call a werewolf."

9

I barked out a laugh. It sounded shaky, even to my ears. It was either that or start screaming. "So, you're trying to tell me I'm a werewolf? You're kidding, right? That's just some sort of weird code word for you people who like to live out here in the forest."

Ranger looked at me as if I should know better, then shook his head.

"Well, you don't mean a *werewolf*, right?"

"Oh, but I do. Only we prefer the term *lycanthrope*. Or *shape-shifter*. Or better yet, *Lycanthian*."

Speechless, I stared at him, sure this was some horrible joke. Finally, I found my voice. "You mean like in the movies, under the full moon, I'll turn into some kind of raving wolf maniac and can't be killed except with a silver bullet?" I snorted in disbelief.

"The werewolf you describe is mostly a product of man's imagination. A warped perspective, to say the least. But those shifters who have no pack to turn to for guidance or help can become those kinds of creatures. This"—he waved his hand to indicate the village, the entire forest surrounding it—"is your home. It's where you and your parents spent the first three years of your life. It is where you belong," he continued, more gently now. "Where you will learn how to accept the gift you've been given."

I'd been so sure going off with Ranger had been the right thing to do. But now everything had gone sour, twisted. It was just plain wrong.

"Your mother was one of the few humans who loved our way of life. She and your father were extremely happy here."

"So then what happened? Why don't I still live here?"

"When you were three years old, your mother became ill. Your father took her back to the city for medical treatment. She never recovered fully, so your father thought it best to stay in the city, close to the doctors she would need. He was very good at passing among humans."

"And then?"

Ranger turned and stared off into the distance. "And then they died." A spasm of grief passed over his face. "In a car accident. And then I came for you, as I had promised my brother. Only, when I arrived, Stephen and Jane already had you, and they wouldn't let you go. They mounted a court battle, made all sorts of accusations that caused the courts to decide I was an unfit guardian. We, the pack and I, had to back off, no matter how painful the defeat. We couldn't afford to bring that much attention to ourselves. It was too dangerous."

My head reeled. I needed to sit down. I backed up until I bumped into a nearby boulder, parked my backside on it, then drew a shaky breath. The court hadn't wanted to hand a three-year-old over to a pack of werewolves. Yep. Made sense to me. Panic thudded in my chest. I'd possibly just made the biggest mistake of my life.

Ranger's soft voice continued, as if he were afraid to stop talking, stop explaining. "But I swore I would come for you before your thirteenth birthday. And I did, but not a day too soon."

"Why is my thirteenth birthday such a big deal?"

"Every Lycanthian's thirteenth birthday falls on a full moon—in your case, tomorrow night. That's when Lycanthians born of a human mother shift for the first time. It's important to do it in the right place, surrounded by the right energy, or things can go terribly wrong."

I wanted to tell myself he was kidding, or he was stark raving mad, but that's not what his eyes said.

Just then, Ulric came over and laid his hand on Ranger's shoulder, but looked intently at me. "Is everything okay over here?"

Ranger nodded, but didn't look away from me. Maybe he was afraid I would start screaming or something.

Finally, with two intense pairs of eyes on me, I nodded. "Yeah, I guess I'm okay. I need to get this cut taken care of, though. It's pretty deep."

Much to my annoyance, Ulric threw back his head and laughed, a loud rolling sound that made me want to laugh as well. But there was nothing funny going on. I had a wild-wolf scratch that was probably already starting to get infected. And what about rabies?

"You'll be fine," Ulric said and headed toward the village.

Ranger turned back to me. "Look, even now it begins to heal."

I started to protest, then looked down at my arm. He was right. The scratch had already scabbed over, puckering tight as if I'd had it for days.

"That is one of the gifts of being a shifter. Our immune systems are much stronger than an ordinary human's. Your body heals more quickly."

I looked back up at Ranger, and for the first time, it occurred to me that he might be telling the truth. Images from my dream filled my mind. It all fit. In a bizarre, twisted way.

"What is it, Luc? This strikes some chord in you. I can see it in your eyes."

"A . . . a dream I had. That's all. I've had it for weeks now, and there's this horrible beast in it, and in my dream I wake up, but the beast stays, because he's me. The beast, I mean."

Ranger nodded. "And that's how it could have gone if I hadn't found you in time." He sighed a huge sigh, full of remorse, regret, and patience. "Do you need proof, Luc?" For some reason, it almost sounded like a threat.

"Yeah. I do. You can't expect me to believe a story like this without some proof."

Ranger took two steps back, then stood perfectly still, hands at his sides, head bent as if concentrating. "Watch then, and believe."

Slowly, his features began to blur. So did his clothes. Everything about him blurred and shifted, moving around like a human-shaped container full of churning colors and textures. Slowly, the colors re-formed. Ranger's head grew longer, his nose and mouth elongated. The hair on his head seemed to bush out more, grow down his neck and back.

His torso thinned and shortened, and his arms lengthened until he dropped to all fours, and the colors swirled around, finally coming to rest.

Before me stood a huge, black wolf with piercing, golden eyes.

I gave an involuntary squeak. I would have screamed if I hadn't been so close to hyperventilating. The wolf padded toward me, his eyes compelling me to stand firm, not run. He stopped just in front of me, his rich, thick fur inviting me to run my hands through it.

Almost of its own will my hand crept forward until my fingers felt the soft fur. The wolf—Ranger—leaned forward and nudged me with his cool, wet nose, like a playful dog wanting a rub between the ears. Bolder now, I buried my entire hand in the fur around his neck and rubbed. His wide mouth relaxed into a grin, and I scratched harder until his tongue lolled over to the side.

I was petting a real, live wolf! And not just a wild wolf, but a werewolf. I shivered slightly, but the wolf reached forward and rubbed his muzzle against my shoulder. "Ranger?" I whispered, uncertain and fearful, yet filled with wonder. "Is that really you?"

Catching me off guard, the wolf reached forward and licked my face with his tongue. I made a noise halfway between a laugh and a yuck, and pushed him away.

The wolf stepped back and planted his haunches on the ground, waiting for something.

Have you ever had to crack a knuckle, or your neck, to put it back in place? Well, looking at Ranger in wolf form made it feel like my whole world had just cracked back into place. As if on a deep level I'd known all this, but had forgotten it somehow. Although, how I could forget something like being a werewolf escaped me. But deep in my bones, this whole crazy thing felt right.

"Okay. I believe you. You can change back now."

Before the words were out of my mouth, he began changing. This time the colors and textures, bones and flesh, swirled until they formed the tall, lean shape of Ranger. My uncle. A shape-shifter.

Somewhere, deep inside, a thrill ran through me. "And you're telling me I can do that?"

Ranger nodded. "Starting tomorrow night. We'll have the Transformation Ceremony, and you will change for the first time, with all your pack around you to welcome you to the joys of your wolf shape."

"Unbelievable." I sat on my boulder and tried to digest all this. "Everyone here in this village can do that?"

Ranger nodded. "With the exception of one or two full-blooded human spouses, yes."

This was big. Huge. Something I would never have dreamed up in a million years.

But I *had* dreamed it! Maybe the dreams had only seemed like nightmares because I didn't understand. And it explained so much! All the changes I'd been going through during the last week: my sense of smell, my increased speed.

I must have still looked dazed because Ranger said, "Come on. I will take you to Teague, the pack's bard. He can fill you in on the history of Lycanthians much better than I. Besides, there is a lot to learn before the ceremony tomorrow night, and he's a good place to start."

I stood up, and Ranger put his arm around my shoulders. The easy gesture of acceptance felt surprisingly good.

As we walked through the middle of the village, I expected the whole world to look different. As if now that I knew the truth, it would affect how I saw everything. There were only a few people around, and no wolves, much to my disappointment. Now that I knew, I wanted to see more of them. Suddenly a thought occurred to me. "That was you I saw last night outside the motel window!"

Ranger gave a little smile. "Yes. After being in the city for any length of time, I can hardly wait to shift back to my wolf form. To run off the discomfort of being where the buildings are too close together, there are too many people, and the air reeks of gasoline."

"And the diner last night? All those weird looks?"

"That was another Lycanthian village. Those that live the closest to human cities are the most cautious."

"But that wolf that attacked me. If I am part of his pack, why did he attack me like that?"

Ranger smiled. "Nuri is young and hotheaded. He didn't intend to hurt you, merely to welcome you and confirm his superior position within the pack."

"A simple sentence or two would have worked just fine," I said.

Ranger laughed. "I would agree. But Nuri's only been in full possession of all his wolf powers for a year. They are still amazing and new to him, and he doesn't have complete control over them yet." He turned and looked at me. "It will be the same for you."

Terrific. And I had thought having no control over my hormones was going to be bad. This could prove to be a whole lot worse.

We headed toward one of the buildings that was larger than the others. "The schoolhouse," Ranger explained. As we drew near, a man appeared in the doorway. He was older, with short silver hair and a neat trimmed beard.

"Ah!" he said, when he spotted us. "I was just coming to find you. I heard you'd arrived."

Ranger smiled. "And here we are. Teague, this is Luc."

Teague frowned slightly. "There were no problems, I trust?"

"None that need to be discussed now," Ranger said with a meaningful glance at me.

"Very well." Teague turned his striking, pale blue eyes to me. I wondered if they stayed that color when he shifted. "Perhaps you'd like to walk for a while after your long car ride. I can tell you a little something about us."

"Whatever you wish," Ranger said.

Teague put his hand on my shoulder and steered Ranger and me toward the village. "You have much of your grandfather in you," he said.

I whipped my head around to Ranger. "Grandfather? I have a grandfather?"

Ranger smiled. "Yes. His name is Sterling. He and Teague are fierce competitors at chess."

"When can I meet him?"

"When you are through here, we will pay him a visit."

"But can't I go see him first? I mean, he is my grandfather."

Ranger shook his head. "He is your grandfather, but

Teague is of higher rank in the pack, and so you must see him first."

I opened my mouth to argue, but Ranger interrupted me.

"It is our way. You must learn to accept it."

Well, we'd see about that. But for now I let it go.

The matter settled to his satisfaction, Teague began speaking. "We Lycanthians are a very old race, Luc, dating back to ancient Rome. The power to shift between wolf form and human form was granted to us then, as a gift of appreciation. Lupa, the mother of all Lycanthians, had found two babies in the woods, you see, and took them as her own so they would not suffer and perish. You are familiar with Roman mythology, yes?"

I nodded. "We covered it in sixth grade."

"Then you know these two babies as Romulus and Remus, the founders of Rome. As a thank-you gift from the gods, the ability to shift between shapes was granted to Lupa and her descendants. This gift was to assist us in our position as protectors of man."

"B-but mythology isn't real," I sputtered. "It's like fairy tales."

"Oh, it's real. At least some of it."

As I considered this new twist on Roman history, I spied two wolves romping around, nipping at each other and wrestling over in a clearing. I couldn't tell if they were playing or fighting. Either way, it was nearly impossible to believe they were also human.

"Lycanthians thrived," Teague's voice continued, "until the Middle Ages and the Inquisition and witch hunts. Our ability to shift was seen as a sorcerer's trick, something given to us by the devil, not the gift from God that it was. Neighbors, terrified of being persecuted themselves, swore under oath that they had seen us do vile things in our lust for human flesh. It wasn't true. None of it. Oh, there may have been the occasional rogue Lycanthian, but no more so than when a murderer or serial killer shows up in the human population."

The idea of a werewolf serial killer made me shiver. Or maybe it was the sight of the wolves over in the clearing. They were definitely fighting, and I couldn't help but remember a set of wolfish teeth inches from my face just a short while ago.

Just then, another wolf approached the two, head bowed. This one had fur that was either a light silver or white, I couldn't quite tell. The others were so intent on their fight that they ignored it. Ever so gently, the third wolf reached in with its nose and nudged the flank of the wolf who seemed to be winning the skirmish.

In a flash, the fighting wolf turned on the silver one, lips pulled back, teeth bared. A vicious growl came deep from within his throat.

Teague's hand clamped down on my shoulder as he tried to steer me away from the clearing. Ranger was still watching. Teague cleared his throat, and Ranger turned back around.

The older man sighed heavily. "Wolves and lycanthropes are no more inherently evil than man, perhaps less so. We certainly lack man's talent for bigotry and persecution. Instead of being able to protect man, we've become his most feared nightmare, through no fault of our own."

At this point, the growling and yipping behind us grew so loud I turned around again. There was a full-blown wolf fight going on.

I turned to see what Ranger thought of this, but he was already heading for the clearing.

"Ranger! Wait!" Teague called after him. "Do not interfere."

But Ranger had shifted into his wolf form.

10

The silver wolf was flat on her back, fending off a full attack by the other two. One took a powerful swipe at her flank, while the other grabbed her by the throat and took her head down to the ground.

Like a streaking black missile, Ranger launched himself at the wolf whose teeth were buried in the silver one's neck. He struck it and sent them both tumbling. There was a vicious snapping of jaws, deep-throated growls, and then Ranger had one of the attacking wolves flat on the ground. He snarled viciously at the second one, who crouched on his belly, muzzle bowed in submission.

The silver wolf rolled to her side and watched, but didn't try to get away. Teague strode out into the action, his voice cutting through the wolf noises. "Ranger! Get off Rolfe. You cannot interfere like this."

I looked at Teague in surprise. "Why not?" I asked. "They were beating the crap out of the silver wolf!" I would think that was one of the advantages to being a big, powerful wolf: putting bullies in their place.

Teague glared at me briefly. Power rose off of him like steam, and for a minute, I thought he was going to come after me. Then he turned his attention back to Ranger. He completely ignored the silver wolf on the ground.

"This is not your concern, Ranger," he said in a voice that made me want to crawl on my belly and beg forgiveness, even though I had done nothing.

Or maybe that's what I wanted to ask forgiveness for, standing there and doing nothing.

With a ripple of power and a swirl of colors, shapes, and textures, Ranger returned to his human form. He tossed one more condemning glare at the two cringing wolves he had bested and went to the silver wolf. He knelt beside her. "Are you all right, Luna?"

The air rippled again, and there was a swirl of silvers and light gray, then a woman sat on the ground where the wolf had been.

She had pale blond hair, almost white, that went halfway down her back. Her eyes were gray, so light and shimmering they almost looked silver. She pushed herself to a sitting position, gasped, and put her hands to her rib cage.

"You're hurt," Ranger said. He reached out and gently checked her for bumps and bruises. When his hand made contact with the deep claw marks on her arm, she cried out a little, and he growled low in his throat.

"Really, Ranger. I'm fine," she said, looking nervously at Teague.

Ranger glared over his shoulder at the two young

wolves, now in their human shape. "But you wouldn't have been if they'd kept going."

The two guys stood huddled together, heads bowed, not meeting anyone's eyes. One was about my size, maybe a little heavier. The other was taller and had kind of a harsh look to him.

Luna looked up at Ranger, her eyes full of sorrow and a mild reproach. "Still, you shouldn't have interfered. I am Omega. This is my position in the pack, to—"

"Be their whipping boy?" he asked, the anger still deep and strong in his voice.

"Their what?" Luna asked, not understanding.

Ranger shook his head. "Never mind. Here, let me help you up." For someone who said she was fine, she leaned heavily on Ranger as she struggled to her feet.

Teague watched with his jaw clenched. He turned to the two boys. "Go on now, off with you. Surely you have something more productive to do than this. The woodpile was looking very low this morning. If all else fails you can chop some wood."

As they slunk off, the taller one, the one that looked like he ate nails for breakfast, threw a look over his shoulder that held shame, and something else. Something a little more frightening. A promise of vengeance, maybe.

Teague turned to Ranger, his voice small and tight. "What do you think you're doing? Have you moved among humans so much that you've forgotten?"

Ranger glared at the older man. "I've forgotten nothing except how much I hate young bullies taking out their aggression on the Omega when it can be put to better use.

Especially those two. They're always looking for a reason to hammer those weaker than themselves."

The older man sucked in a breath. "That is the Omega's *job*. That is her position in the pack. Nothing you can do or say will change that. It is the way it has always been and will always be. She accepts it; why can't you?" He turned to Luna, who was still standing next to Ranger. "Go see Kora if you need to."

Luna nodded, threw one last glance at Ranger, then hurried off.

"I will accompany her—" Ranger began, but Teague cut him off.

"Stop! You will not accompany the Omega. What kind of example are you setting?" He nodded in my direction. I had to fight down the urge to tell him not to drag me into this. I hadn't liked watching the wolves beat up on Luna any more than Ranger had.

Ranger stared at Teague for a second longer, the air filled with his disgust and frustration. Finally, just when I was certain the air between the two would burst into flame, Ranger turned and strode away, calling for me to follow. I hurried after him, anxious to be away from Teague.

"Hey," I called out. He slowed his pace enough for me to catch up. "Why are those guys allowed to beat her up like that?" I asked.

"Because she is Omega," Ranger said, as though that explained everything. "Last in the pack."

"And that makes it okay to use her as a punching bag?"

Ranger stopped walking and turned to face me. I could tell he was mad, but I could also tell he wasn't mad at me. "She must be submissive to all. Whenever anybody feels like demonstrating their dominance or aggression, she has no choice but to accept their behavior."

I swallowed. Sounded like a lousy job to me. "Is she being punished for something?"

"No. It is simply her job. Ever since her Day of Choosing nearly ten years ago." He began walking again, and so did I.

"She didn't choose *that*, did she?" I couldn't imagine *anyone* choosing a job like that.

"No," Ranger said. "She didn't. But they didn't like what she did choose, so they gave her that instead."

11

I followed Ranger back through the village. I wanted to stop and examine the cabins that looked as if they'd been built with Lincoln Logs and stones, but I had to hurry to keep up.

When he turned toward the door of a wooden cabin, I couldn't stand it any longer. "So, which is my grandfather's house?"

Ranger threw me an impatient glance. "That one there." He pointed to the farthest end of the village.

"There're three. Which one is his?"

The stiffness in his face and shoulders relaxed a little as he remembered that I knew nothing about life out here. "The one with the gray stone. The village is laid out according to pack dominance," he explained. "The houses near the entrance belong to those highest in the pack. That way, in case of attack, we can defend the village. The elders aren't as able to assist in hunting and protecting the pack, so they live down there." Then pointed to the cabin across from his.

"That's where Ulric and his wife, Sasha, live. On the other side is Niall's house. He's the Beta, second only to Ulric." He opened his front door and impatiently motioned me inside.

"What's your position in the pack?"

Ranger closed the door and shrugged out of his coat. "I am Fenriki," he said, as if that explained everything.

It didn't. "You used that word before. What does it mean?"

He tossed his coat on the couch and went to peer out the front window. "It's part diplomatic agent, part secret police. I answer only to Ulric and am not part of the traditional pack structure."

"Oh."

Ranger turned from the window. "Let me show you your room."

He led me through a nearly empty living room (no TV! no stereo!) to a just-as-bare spare bedroom. It had only a bed, a wooden desk, and a closet.

"Now," he said, turning away from me, "I have things to do. Go ahead and make yourself comfortable."

"Yeah, I'll go unpack my things," I said.

Before Ranger could laugh at my feeble attempt at humor, there was a knock on the door. Ranger crossed the room, almost as if he were glad for the interruption. "There's my summons."

Summons? *Summons?* That made Ulric sound like a . . . a dictator or something.

"Ulric and I must talk about increasing the patrols now that"—his gaze flickered to me then away again—"now that I've returned. Stay here. When I get back I'll take you to meet your grandfather."

That was fine with me. After having just been dropped into the middle of the Twilight Zone, I didn't mind a little time alone to do some thinking.

Or so I thought. But my mind was clocking along at about a hundred miles an hour. I needed some way to turn it off, and there was absolutely nothing to do. No TV, no computer, no radio, nothing. I tried pacing, but that didn't work, so I plopped onto the couch and tried to make some sense out of what I'd learned today. I could handle everything up till the werewolf—excuse me—*Lycanthian* part. Every time I came up against that, it was like my mind slammed into a brick wall.

I jumped up off the couch and went to look out the living-room window. There was no sign of Ranger, but if I smashed my face up against the glass and twisted my neck, I could just make out the corner of my grandfather's house. I sighed in frustration. Ranger didn't really expect me to sit here and twiddle my thumbs, did he? Not with a grandfather just a few doors down.

All of my life there had been a great gaping hole where my father's family should have been. I had thought they were all dead. A huge bubble of anger rose up from my gut. Stephen had no right to keep all of this from me. I would never be able to forgive him for this.

I took a few deep breaths and tried to get a grip on my temper. I wasn't used to having a temper, and I wasn't sure I liked it. Then I realized I could just *go*. I could just open the freakin' door and do it. So I did.

Luckily, all the cabins were half buried in trees and bushes, so it was pretty easy to get from one end of the village to the other without being seen. But the closer I got to my grandfather's house, the more I hung back. I wanted to see him, but I was nervous. I mean, what was I going to say to him once I'd met him? A grandfather I didn't even remember having?

When I reached the house, I couldn't quite bring myself to march right up and knock on the front door. I decided to go around to the back and sort of scope out the territory.

I pushed my way through shoulder-high shrubs until I reached the backyard. An older man puttered in the garden. My grandfather? I wiped my sweaty palms on my pants.

He pulled a few weeds out of the ground, then stood up and turned in my direction. I jerked back under the shadow of the trees, but he hadn't spotted me. He went to get the hose, then turned back to the plants.

Once I'd seen his face, it was easy to tell that he was Ranger's father. He had the same strong nose and deep-set eyes. The shape of him was similar, and he had the same pride in his bearing that Ranger had.

As I stood there spying on him, a thought hit me like a sledgehammer. This is how my father would have looked in twenty years. If he had lived. That blew me away. It was like looking at an alternate reality.

"Hello," my grandfather said without turning around. His voice was rich and deep and had me gasping in surprise.

"How . . . but . . . I never . . ."

"You're upwind," he said. He let go of the hose, and slowly turned around, as if he were afraid I might run away if he moved too quickly. When our eyes met, I could see a jolt of recognition run through him, and he looked as if he'd seen a ghost. "Luc," he said, his voice gruff with emotion.

I took a few steps closer.

"You're the spitting image of your father."

"Really?" It was embarrassing how starved I was for this kind of information.

He nodded. Then, as if unable to resist any longer, he stepped forward and pulled me into a massive hug. I was swamped by a sense of strength and wisdom. And acceptance. Bone-deep acceptance. It was like I had just discovered a vital body part that I hadn't known was missing.

When he pulled out of the hug, his eyes were a little moist. Luckily, I had stopped doing the moist-eye thing back when I was eleven, otherwise I would have embarrassed myself.

"Come on," he finally said. "Let's go inside."

His house was smaller than Ranger's but had lots more stuff in it. As my grandfather cleared a place for us to sit, he kept staring at me as if I were a genie who had just popped out of a bottle and he half expected me to disappear again.

He sat down. "So, tell me a little about yourself," he said, sounding almost hungry.

I gave him the short version, about my grades and classes, my friends, what sports I liked to watch. I left out the part about being the Pierpoint Middle School weenie up until a week ago. There were some things even a grandfather didn't need to know. I ran out of things to say pretty quickly. My life really hadn't been very interesting up until a few days ago. Honest.

"So," I said, clasping my hands together, "now it's your turn."

"Well, I used to be the pack's Alpha until about nine years ago." His face kind of drooped for a moment, then went back to normal. It didn't take a genius to do the math here. "I knew it was time to hand over the ruling of the pack to someone else, someone stronger, less dispirited than myself. Ulric was next in the royal line."

Whoa. "Royal line?"

"Yes. Only those with royal blood can be a ruling Alpha. Ulric is my nephew. That would make him your"—he paused for a moment and tried to figure it out—"second cousin, maybe?"

"So you—we—have royal blood as well?"

Sterling nodded. "You could very well end up being this pack's ruling Alpha in due time."

"Uh, no thanks." I was having a hard enough time getting used to just the Lycanthian part. "What about Ranger?"

"Oh, him, too. He was only twenty-five when I stepped down, not old enough or wise enough to rule. He could also be Alpha someday, if he wanted. But I think he likes being Fenriki. He seems to enjoy the challenges of passing in the human world."

My grandfather stood. "Would you like to see some pictures of your father?"

I nodded, then followed him down the hall into a room that was crowded with old junk.

I studied the photos on the wall while my grandfather rummaged through the albums on the shelf. I saw a picture of my father standing in cap and gown and holding a diploma.

"Here we go," my grandfather's voice called out. I went over to stand next to him. He pointed to a picture in the album. "See? Like enough to be twins."

He was right. Except for the out-of-style clothes and a slightly different haircut, it could have been me. I reached out and ran my finger over the picture.

Sterling cleared his throat. "There's more. Lots more. Feel free to look through the whole book." He handed the album to me.

I bent down and pored over the pages. There was a picture of my father taking his first step, sitting under a Christmas tree next to an infant who had to be Ranger. I saw snapshots of my dad fishing, sitting next to a campfire, and working on a wood project. I turned to the next page and stopped.

A wolf's face stared back at me. The fur was somewhere between gray and black, the eyes a striking brilliant green. Like mine.

I looked up. "Is this . . . ?"

He nodded, and I turned back to the picture. No matter how long I looked, there was nothing I recognized. Except for the eyes. They were definitely familiar. Sighing in frustration, I turned the page.

There was a wedding picture of my father and my mother, holding hands in a grove of trees with people gathered all around them. The expression on my mother's face was so happy she glowed. So did my father. Seeing them like that almost hurt.

"Tell me," I said, "was my mother . . . happy?"

My grandfather put a hand on my shoulder. "Look at her face, Luc. She was full of joy. As was Kennet. They were perfect for each other and head over heels in love." There was a catch in his voice. "The only time I ever saw them happier was when you were born. It was as if someone had come along and placed both the sun and the moon right in their lap and they would never want for anything more." He stopped talking, and a sense of grief filled the small room.

I traced my hand over the picture again, relieved to hear

how happy she had been. "Stephen, my uncle, never told me that. Only how hard her life had been. I'm glad to know she was happy."

At the mention of Stephen's name, the whole atmosphere in the room seemed to change, as if storm clouds had just come through the door. I glanced up, surprised to see a look of fury on my grandfather's face. I was swamped with an urge to fall at his feet and beg forgiveness. Although for what, I had no idea. This whole groveling-urge-thing was new to me.

"Stephen." Sterling spat out the word as if something nasty and bitter had found its way onto his tongue. "Do not speak his name in this house."

"Right. Sorry." I should have guessed he'd feel that way. I groped around for a neutral topic. "Is there a picture of my grandmother in here?"

My grandfather took a few deep breaths and his color went back down to normal. He reached around me and turned a few pages in the album then stepped back. I was looking into a smiling face with warm eyes.

"She died shortly after Kennet," Sterling said, staring out the window. "A group of hunters came into our midst. She let herself be taken so that the others could make their escape." His eyes stared out the window at some long-remembered horror. Slowly, he turned and met my gaze. Raw heart-wrenching pain filled the room. "I was away at the time, tending to some . . . business, surrounding Kennet's death. I will never forgive myself for not being by her side, protecting her."

A door opened, and Sterling said under his breath, "Ranger's here."

"Hello?" Ranger's voice called out. "Anyone home?"

"We're in here," Sterling called out.

Ranger appeared in the doorway, glowering at me.

I gave a weak smile. "How did you know I was here?"

"Nine different people saw you walk here from my house."

So much for being sneaky.

He continued to stare at me until I wanted to squirm. "Next time I tell you to wait, you wait. Got that?"

"Got it," I said, mortified to be chewed out in front of my grandfather.

"So I see you were successful," my grandfather said, drawing Ranger's attention away from me.

Ranger nodded. "In a manner of speaking, yes."

All sorts of unspoken things zoomed between them, but they said nothing more out loud. Finally, Ranger turned to me. "Come," he said. "We need to get ready for the dinner. Your grandfather will be there and you can talk more then."

12

As Ranger and I left for the Great Hall, I tried not to be nervous about meeting an entire pack of werewolves all at once. I wasn't succeeding.

"It's just a dinner to welcome you into the pack," Ranger explained. "You aren't required to make a speech or anything. You're not even the main course."

"Ha ha. Very funny." But of course that was just a little bit on my mind. I mean, they *were* werewolves, and everything I'd ever heard about them indicated they were bloodthirsty and violent, with a special love of chomping on humans.

Ranger continued. "Niall, Sloan, and Killian went out hunting earlier today in honor of your dinner. They managed to catch a deer and an elk, so we'll be eating well tonight."

"I wish they hadn't done that." *I will* not *get sick. I will* not *get sick*, I chanted to myself over my rising nausea. I could hardly believe I'd managed to choke down a cheeseburger last night. I definitely wasn't ready for food that had been dead less than four hours. Eating Bambi, especially fresh Bambi, grossed me out.

"How else would you like us to get food?"

"The grocery store?"

Ranger snorted. "There is no honor in buying a piece of cow from the refrigerated section of a grocery store."

"Yeah, but there's no bloodshed, either."

Ranger looked amused. "How do you think the cow came to be on the shelf, then?"

"Well, no bloodshed that I had to be a part of."

"Exactly. That is the coward's way out. For Lycanthians, hunting is a sacred act. We honor and respect the life that we take by wasting nothing.

"But, either way, do your best to eat up. It will be one of your last meals before your change tomorrow night."

"It will?"

Ranger nodded. "After breakfast tomorrow, you will have to fast."

"I won't be able to eat for the whole day?" I asked, hungry just thinking about it.

He shook his head.

I thought for a moment. "In order to purify my body and focus my mind on the important changes to come?" I asked.

Ranger turned and looked at me, trying not to smile. "Not exactly. Changing for the first time will make you dizzy and disoriented. If you eat during the day, you will puke it all up during the change. Messy business, that. Sort of spoils the moment."

Uh, yeah. I'll say.

"Besides, you'll be too nervous to be hungry." Then he

gave me a wolfish smile and opened the door to the Great Hall, where the entire village waited for us. "Oh, and remember," he added. "To refuse to eat the meat from a wolf's table is a grave insult."

Well, that seemed kind of important to know. Was I going to be able to survive my own ignorance?

Ranger held the door open for me, and I stepped into the Great Hall. Blazing candlelight, raised voices, and the smell of roasting meat were my first impressions of the room. Five enormous tables ran nearly the full length of the hall, with the middle table raised higher than the others. A fireplace took up the entire south wall. Three great chairs—thrones really—sat in front of the fireplace on a raised platform of some sort. The windows were all of colored glass and showed wolves and trees and rocks in colors as rich as jewels.

I looked up at the ceiling, which was constructed of massive beams that looked as though they had been hewn from ancient trees. Hanging from these beams were large hoops of iron that held hundreds of candles, all lit and burning brightly. More candleholders jutted out from the walls, each of them full of at least a dozen burning candles.

Ranger led me to the raised middle table, where Ulric stood talking to a man and a woman. The woman was tall, nearly as tall as Ulric. Her hair was long and dark, with a white streak running through it. When she turned to me and our eyes met, a small jolt went through me. Her eyes were yellow. Not a deep gold or amber like Ranger's, but an eerie cat's-eye yellow.

Ulric reached out and clasped me in a giant bear hug that forced all of the air out of my lungs in a big *whoosh*. Or would that be *wolf* hug? I needed some time to figure that one out.

"Welcome, Luc, son of Kennet and Sara! I hear you have met your grandfather today."

Sheesh. Absolutely no secrets.

"Let me introduce you to those who weren't in the village this morning when you arrived."

He turned to the woman next to him. "This is our priestess, Sasha. She's also my wife."

"Welcome, Luc." Her voice was low and warm and reminded me of hot chocolate. She leaned forward to kiss both my cheeks, and for some reason I thought of earth and leaves and growing things.

"Pleased to meet you," I managed to stammer out.

"Here are Loki and Torin," Ulric said, indicating two men off to his right. "They were out harvesting when you arrived. And Rhea here missed you earlier because she was watching the pups." The next minutes were spent in a confusing jumble of names, hands to be shaken, and cheeks to be kissed. *Here, Luc. I'd like you to meet TorinRheaSilasKora-LiamWandaLokiRamonaShawnaKevinandTraci.* Like I was ever going to remember them all!

Even worse, everyone who greeted me touched me. Some patted my head, others stroked my arm, a few put their arm around my shoulders, and still others rubbed the top of my head. I tried to remember the last time Uncle Stephen had touched me, and came up empty.

As I stood there trying not to look stupid, a soft voice whispered in my ear. "Don't worry. There won't be a quiz later."

"Thank God!" I turned around and found myself staring into a pair of dancing silver eyes.

"Hello. We haven't been properly introduced, but I'm Luna."

I reached out to shake her hand. "Hi. Ranger's told me a lot about you."

She smiled at the mention of Ranger's name, and little dimples flashed in her cheeks.

"Welcome to the pack." She gave a little wave, then disappeared back into the crowd, and I was standing all alone again in a group of strangers. *Pack,* I corrected myself. *Family.*

I tried to pay attention to their conversation, but it was all meaningless to me. I tuned out their voices and pulled a chair from the table, intending to sit down, yelping when a large hand grabbed me by the collar.

I looked up to find Ulric staring at me, steely-eyed. "You stand until those more dominant sit, or you ask permission." His voice was lethally quiet.

I gulped. "Sorry." I pushed the chair back in and stood up. Only now I was a lot less bored and a lot more nervous. Everyone around here was way too hung up on power trips.

A few minutes later, Ulric strode to the front of the room and leaped up onto the platform in front of the roaring fire. He stood for a minute, pride and leadership oozing from every cell in his body. Finally, he raised his head and made a sound halfway between a snarl and a bark.

All the hairs along my arms stood up at attention. Everyone quieted down immediately and went to stand behind a chair.

Ulric began speaking. "We are gathered here tonight to welcome Luc, son of Kennet and Sara, grandson to Sterling, and nephew to Ranger, into our pack."

A murmur of pleasure went up from the tables.

"He has spent his whole life believing himself to be human," Ulric continued. "Therefore, he has much to learn. You will all need to be patient, attentive teachers."

Several nods and voices of assent rippled through the room like a small fierce wind. Those closest to me thumped me on the back or patted me on the shoulder.

"Tomorrow is the full moon of Luc's thirteenth birthday. So tonight, we not only welcome Luc into our pack, but celebrate his upcoming transformation. Let's bow our heads."

We all bowed.

Ulric continued. "We offer our thanks, both to the gods of old for granting us our gift, and to the One God for blessing us with the keeping of it. We are honored by the trust placed in us and vow to uphold it with our lives. We are thankful, also, for the prey that honors our table. Their gift is great and we will treat it with respect and honor for all the days of our lives. Amen."

Then Ulric's deep voice boomed out over the room. "A toast," he declared, "to our newest member!" He reached down and grabbed a cup that had been on a small table near his chair. He lifted the goblet high into the air. All around me the Lycanthians lifted their goblets. Ranger nodded to mine, indicating that I should take it. I picked it up and found it was carved horn, or antlers maybe, and filled with deep red liquid. For one horrid moment, I thought it might be blood, until I realized it was too thin and smelled sharply of grapes.

"To Luc," Ulric cried. "May your pelt be thick, your hunt plentiful, and your soul filled with the honor of your pack."

Everyone around me raised their glasses and took a drink. I looked at Ranger, uncertain what to do. He motioned for me to drink, so I did.

I was right. It was some kind of grape juice, but with a sharp tang to it.

"Let the feast begin!" Ulric jumped down from the platform and took his place at the head of the table. As if on cue, we all sat.

I felt a nudge on my arm and an enormous platter was shoved at me. I took it and found myself looking down at big chunks of deer meat swimming in some kind of sauce. I glanced up to find Ranger watching me with a raised eyebrow.

I put some of the stuff on my plate and passed the platter to him. With his comment about grave insults still ringing in my ears, I held my breath and dug in.

To keep my mind off of what I was chewing, I looked around the room. None of the kids sat with their families. Instead, they all sat in a group at the lower end of the farthest table. Older people, my grandfather's age, sat at the other end of the same table.

In between the elders and the juveniles sat Luna, almost as if she were a boundary line. As if sensing me staring, she turned and raised her glass to me in a private toast. I smiled back, feeling the nervousness and pressure inside calm down a little. Her eyes shifted and looked next to me. I looked up to find Ranger staring at her.

Ranger caught me watching him and flushed slightly before turning back to his dinner.

He had a thing for her! Finally, a chink in that armor of his. Smiling to myself, I took another bite of dead-deer meat.

The man sitting next to me saw me smiling. "Ah," he said, smiling back. "You already have a taste for our food. Good!" And before I could say a word, he heaped another pile of the nasty stuff on my plate.

13

When dinner was over, Ulric turned to me. "Why don't you join the other juveniles, Luc. Ranger and I need to talk."

I glanced over my shoulder and saw all of the younger members of the pack sitting together. They'd obviously known one another forever. The idea of trying to barge in on their little group made my heart thump and my palms sweat.

I turned back around. "I'll pass. I don't—"

A low growl started in Ulric's throat, his lips pulling back just the littlest bit. He went from Benign Leader to Threatening Bully in under two seconds.

Ranger put his hand on my shoulder. "You must do as Ulric commands."

Commands? I thought as I stood up. *What's with this freaking command stuff? It's not like he's a king or something.* I suddenly realized I didn't really know that. For all I knew, Ulric could actually *be* king of the Lycanths. Hadn't Sterling said he had royal blood? Terrific. Had I just traded Herr Commandant Stephen for King Ulric? I hoped not. I was quickly learning that I preferred a more democratic form of government.

As I walked across the room, I did my best to ignore the dozens of eyes watching me. Most were friendly, but as the small hairs along my neck prickled, I realized one or two felt hostile. Which made no sense. I was the most vulnerable one in the room.

When I reached the far table, the "juveniles" fell silent and turned to stare at me. I stood there like an idiot, not knowing what to do next. I don't know if Luna could tell how miserable I was or if she was just always polite, but she scooted her chair back and stood up. "Hello, Luc. Come meet the others." She gestured to the group at the table.

A girl with a long curtain of black hair and the palest green eyes I had ever seen smiled. "Hello, Luc."

As I looked into her exotic, silver-green eyes, I wondered how I could ever have mistaken these people for normal humans. I cleared my throat. Twice. "Uh, hi."

"Luc, this is Suki," Luna said, nodding her head to the girl who'd just spoken.

"You should be introducing me first," a belligerent voice interrupted. It was one of the guys I'd seen attack Luna earlier in the day. "My dad's higher in the pack than Suki's."

His buddy sitting next to him snickered. Suki took her eyes from me and quietly looked down at the table in front of her.

Luna answered in a calm voice. "You are all juveniles until your Day of Choosing, Rolfe, and therefore equals until that time. Besides"—she smiled, trying to appease him—"Suki greeted him first."

"Actually," a cheerful voice interrupted. "I greeted him first." I turned and saw a kid about my age. He sat twitching and bouncing in his chair as if sitting still were physically impossible for him. He looked familiar.

"Yes, Nuri. I heard about that." Again Luna smiled, clearly relieved to change the subject.

Nuri! "You're the one who knocked me on my butt when I first got here. The one Ulric—"

"Took to the ground. Yup. That was me." He didn't look the slightest bit embarrassed about his public screwup. I had to admire a guy like that.

"And this is Rolfe," Luna continued, finally getting around to Mr. Full-of-Himself.

I nodded at him, determined to be polite. "Hey."

He tilted his head and peered down his nose at me. "Hay is for horses," he said arrogantly.

Hel-lo. That was the oldest joke on the planet. The one we all learned back in preschool.

Luna the peacemaker stepped in. "Perhaps where Luc comes from it is a perfectly acceptable form of greeting." Rolfe shot her a poisonous look.

Trying to lighten things up a bit, I looked back toward the room where the adults sat. "So which one is your dad?" I asked Rolfe.

The guy pulled back his lips. "He's not here. Niall either. They had to take patrol duty tonight."

"Really? What are they patrolling for?"

Silence filled the space around me. Rolfe opened his mouth to say something, but Luna gave a quick shake of her head. Reluctantly, he shut his mouth.

"And this is Wiley," Luna continued as if Rolfe weren't glaring daggers at her.

I grinned. "As in Coyote?" I asked, anxious to connect with these people who were as alien to me as, well, aliens.

Wiley leaped to his feet, shoving his chair back. "Are you calling me a coyote?" He made a spitting motion off to the side. "A pathetic scavenger?"

"No! It was only a joke. Like Wile E. Coyote in the Roadrunner cartoons." I glanced around uneasily; his outbreak had drawn the attention of some of the adults. Just what I needed, to piss off a room full of werewolves.

Apparently, humor was not their strong point.

"Oh, cartoons!" The girl sitting next to Suki clapped her hands. "I love cartoons."

There was a murmur of agreement at the table. Okay, they did know what cartoons were. Phew.

Suki gestured to the girl next to her, the one who loved cartoons. "This is Risa."

"Hi," I said, not about to get into the whole "hey" thing again.

Risa smiled. "Hey." Her warm brown eyes crinkled at the corners.

I heard a snort from Rolfe and Wiley's direction, but I ignored it. "So, which cartoons do you like?" I asked.

As Risa tilted her head to think for a minute, a tumble of brown curls fell into her face. She brushed them aside impatiently. "I like *Dennis the Menace* and *Peanuts* the best."

I frowned. "Oh! You mean comics. You like comic strips. In the newspaper."

Her face fell. "Did I say it wrong?" She looked worried, and I felt awful for having pointed out her mistake.

"Well, kind of. Comics are like cartoons, but on paper. Actual cartoons are the ones on TV or videos or DVDs."

"Oh." She closed her eyes briefly and her lips moved, as if she were committing the words to memory so she wouldn't make that mistake again.

I looked across the table at Nuri. "Do you guys even have TVs or videos or DVDs?"

"We have a television. And videos. But I've never heard of a DVD." He turned with a questioning look to the fellow sitting next to him, who shook his head.

Cripes. "Well, a DVD is a lot like a video, only it's on a CD."

They all had polite-but-blank looks on their faces. "Never mind." I cleared my throat, trying to dislodge the lump of nerves that sat there. "What do you guys do for fun around here?" I decided to let them do the talking. That way I'd end up making fewer mistakes.

"Run around in the forest. Hunt," said Nuri.

"Hunting isn't fun. It's serious work," said an older girl sitting a few chairs down from Nuri.

Nuri shrugged, not in the least bit discouraged about being disagreed with. "It's fun for me," he said.

"Which is why you will never be the hunter I am." The girl tossed her long blond braid over her shoulder.

"This is Killian," Suki explained. "She is one of our best hunters."

Killian gave me a cool nod. "Welcome to the pack."

"Thanks." Ms. Personality she wasn't, but at least she didn't sneer at me. "Is there anything else you like to do besides hunt?"

"The harp," Killian said, her face going all soft and dreamy. "I love to play the harp."

"Ah." I mean, really, what was I supposed to say. *The harp?*

"Well, I love to read the *comics* and play with the cubs," Risa said, putting special emphasis on the word *comics*.

"And you already saw Rolfe and Wiley doing their favorite thing today," Nuri butted in. Then he yelped as Rolfe's foot connected with something tender under the table.

I tried not to flinch as I saw the vicious look Rolfe gave Nuri. I'd have to warn Nuri not to turn his back when Rolfe was around.

Duh. He probably already knew that. I was the one who was going to have to learn not to turn my back on Rolfe.

Wanting to break the tension, I let my gaze wander farther down the table. I saw my grandfather sitting a few chairs down. He looked up from the man he was talking to and winked at me. I grinned back, relieved to have at least one ally.

"Are you just about done here, Luc?" I turned to find Ranger standing behind me. Make that two allies.

"Oh, yeah." I said, standing up. But he wasn't looking at me any longer. He was staring at Luna.

"Hello, Ranger. How is the pack's Fenriki tonight?" she said.

His hands balled into fists. Apparently, he didn't like having her use his title. "Come on, Luc. We have to go."

I followed him toward the door, but before we'd gone more than a few feet, he whispered out of the side of his mouth. "Call Luna. Ask her to come here; say you have a question to ask her."

I looked at him. "If you want me to ask her a question, I'll just run back there—"

"No! Ask her to come here."

"But I hate the way everyone orders her around!"

He heaved an impatient sigh. "I know. And it's one of your better qualities. But I want to talk to her."

Sheesh. Why didn't he just have me pass her a note in homeroom? "Uh, Luna? I have a, er, a question I need to ask you."

Her face was immediately concerned, and she hopped to her feet and hurried over to me and Ranger. I hated how she did that, always scrambling to do whatever anybody demanded.

Luna caught up to us just as we stepped outside. "You needed something?" she asked.

"Well, I . . ." I looked over at Ranger. *Anytime here, big guy.*

He stepped forward. "No. Actually it was I who wanted to talk to you."

It was impossible to tell in the dark, but it felt like she blushed.

I quickly took a few steps toward the village square to put some space between me and Ranger and Luna. The minute I stepped from the porch into the moonlight, my skin started to hum, as if it were attached to some unseen energy force. I glanced up at the moon, now nearly full, its fat round face more mysterious than it had ever been. In the stillness of the night, I could hear the murmur of Ranger and Luna's voices.

Just then, the door to the Great Hall opened, and bright yellow light spilled out. Luna and Ranger jumped apart and turned to see who was coming.

It was Teague. Of course. It was dark enough so that I couldn't see the glare he shot at them, but I could sure feel it. It made me want to squirm and grovel, but I managed to keep still.

"Luc has a big day ahead of him tomorrow, Ranger. Take him back to your cabin and put him to bed. Now," Teague said as he strode past.

Ranger pulled his lips back from his teeth and growled at Teague's back.

Just then, a bone-chilling howl rose up in the night. Ranger froze, and even Teague stopped walking for a moment. But as the howl continued, they all relaxed. "Good," Ranger said. "All is well."

As we headed back to the cabin, I couldn't help but wonder why things wouldn't be well. I mean, werewolves seemed pretty powerful to me. What did they have to fear?

14

I woke up to the sun pouring in through the open curtains and the smell of frying sausages. I jumped out of bed and, realizing I was ravenous, decided to try a new tactic today. I wasn't even going to ask what kind of sausage it was, I was just going to eat it.

There was a pile of clean clothes on the foot of my bed, waiting for me. They weren't mine, and they weren't new, but they were clean, something my clothes hadn't been for a long time. I picked them up and carried them over to the bedroom door. Ranger was rummaging around in the kitchen, and I heard the hiss and sizzle of frying sausage. Moving as quietly as possible, I opened the door.

"You have time for a quick shower before breakfast if you'd like," Ranger called out.

It was going to take some getting used to, this being heard even when I was trying my hardest to be stealthy. I scurried into the bathroom and started the water running. As I waited for it to get hot, I took a quick look in the mirror.

Still exactly the same. Which was pretty disappointing considering I was now thirteen years old *and* a shape-shifter.

By the time I got out of the shower, if felt as if my stomach was eating itself in desperation. I dried off and started to get dressed. The shirt I put on looked vaguely familiar, but where would I have seen it? The feeling of recognition was even stronger as I pulled up the pants. Taking the towel, I wiped the steam off the mirror, then nearly gasped in surprise.

I yanked open the bathroom door and strode into the kitchen. "These are my father's old clothes," I told Ranger.

He lifted an eyebrow at me. "I know," he said as he took sausage links out of the pan he was holding and placed them on two plates.

"But where'd they come from?" I was making too big of a deal out of this, but I couldn't stop myself.

"When Sterling realized you would need clothes to wear, he sent those over."

"Oh." Wearing my dad's clothes was reassuring some-how. Too bad he was such a dorky dresser. His pants had a drawstring waist instead of a zipper or snaps. Then I felt guilty for even thinking the words *dorky* and *father* in the same sentence.

"Breakfast is ready."

"Good. I'm starved." I bit into the sausage, the sweet-spicy taste of it bursting over my tongue and satisfying a craving I didn't even know I had.

All in all, breakfast was going pretty well until Ranger said the dreaded word.

"Lessons?" My heart sank. I had been hoping that being a shape-shifter meant I was going to get out of having to be in school.

Ranger nodded. "Lessons. I told you that the pack is eager for members to learn human skills. Doctors, nurses, teachers, lawyers: all are needed if we are to rise above small groups huddled in remote forests."

"Is that what Lycanthians want?"

"They want to be allowed to live their lives in peace, without being hunted down because of irrational fears or superstitions." Anger crept into Ranger's voice, but he brought it back under control. "In order to do that, we must learn to work within the system. We must be able to appeal to the courts, prove how socialized we really are." He looked up at me with eyes that would accept no argument. "The juveniles meet with Teague in the morning. They are assigned to different adults in the afternoon to help with pack chores and acquire useful life skills." He got up from the table and began clearing the plates. "This afternoon, you meet with Sasha, Teague, and me over at the cairn. We have some things to go over with you before tonight. Now, you need to go or you'll be late. Teague is a stickler for punctuality."

"What's a cairn?"

"Ah. So there is something you don't know, after all," Ranger said. "Maybe you'll find out at school today. Come on." He opened the cabin door and strode out into the morning.

Once again, I followed. I was getting a teensy bit tired of that. I was ready to do some striding of my own.

Ranger pointed down to the end of the village. "Lessons take place in Teague's cottage. Do you remember where that is?"

I nodded.

"So, go. And hurry." He nudged me with his shoulder, and I stepped off the porch and headed down the path that cut through the middle of the village.

The idea of being late and pissing off Teague held a certain appeal, but it also made me nervous. I mean, what kind of punishment did they give out at shape-shifter school?

I walked as fast as I could without breaking into a dead run, but then I looked up to find Teague waiting for me by the door, frowning. All thoughts of dignity fled, and I hustled my butt the last thirty feet or so.

I avoided meeting Teague's eyes as I slunk past him into the room. He shut the door with an efficient little click that managed to sound like a reprimand.

As he strode to the front of the room, he thrust out an arm and pointed to an empty desk. I slid into the chair and tried to pretend I was right on time.

The schoolroom reminded me of an old natural-history museum. Except for the desks, every surface was covered with animal skeletons of all kinds; fish, snakes, small rodents, a wolf, and even a human one, which, by the way the hairs on the back of my neck stood up, I was pretty sure was real.

There was a cluster of old-fashioned microscopes that looked as if they'd been manufactured around 1900, along with maps, a gyroscope, an enormous telescope, and a collection of compasses. There was also a lab area with test tubes, Bunsen burners, and petri dishes. Enormous jars filled with all sorts of nasty-looking things sat on a shoulder-high ledge, and insect collections pinned on boards decorated the walls. Two model airplanes hung suspended from the ceiling as well as two bird skeletons that I couldn't identify.

A huge stuffed owl sat behind Teague's desk. Scattered underneath was a bunch of disgusting little bundles of twigs, hair, and bones. Owl pellets.

There wasn't a computer in sight.

I jumped a little when Teague's voice broke the quietness of the classroom. "What time does school begin, class?" he asked when he reached the front of the room.

"Eight-thirty," everyone chimed in unison.

I slumped down low in my seat.

"I hope we won't have to remind you again, Luc."

"No, sir."

"Good. Now, a few announcements. Our hunting field trip for tomorrow has been postponed until Thursday so that Luc will have a chance to join us."

This was met with a chorus of groans. If I could have slunk lower in my chair without landing on the floor, I would have.

"Then class on Friday will not be held during the day, but we will all meet in the middle of the village at nine-thirty on Friday night for our Navigation with Stars lecture. Any questions?"

No one said anything, so he launched into his lecture. "Since we are of two bodies, it is important that we understand how both of them work. Today we are going to review the liver." Teague reached up and took down two jars filled with something really disgusting. "This is a human liver," he said as he placed the first jar on the desk in front of the human skeleton. "And this," he said, placing an equally disgusting jar in front of the wolf skeleton, "is a wolf liver. Notice the size of the wolf liver, how it is larger than the human liver. This is because the wolf's larger liver is better equipped to handle the large quantities of meat that we consume."

He put his hands behind his back and took a few steps toward the class. "This is also why human doctors often misdiagnose Lycanthians as having liver ailments, when in fact, their liver is just the size it is supposed to be. Which is only one reason we need more Lycanthian doctors. We're counting on some of you to honor your pack in this way." He stared at us all meaningfully. Then he spent the next hour going over all the functions of the liver. It wouldn't have been so bad if I hadn't had to stare at the visual aids the whole time. Looking at the raw livers in the jars made my stomach feel kind of queasy.

I was relieved when he announced it was time for math. I'm *good* at math. Lycanthian anatomy, not so much.

Unfortunately, Teague kept using my math skill to shame the others into understanding a concept. After I answered the third question correctly, Rolfe, Wiley, and Killian turned around and glared at me. Teague either didn't realize he was making the others resent me or he didn't care.

After we put our math books away, we moved on to . . .

"Latin?" I repeated under my breath. Big mistake.

In two long strides, Teague was towering over me, scowling. "Did you say something, Luc?"

I kept forgetting about that wolf-hearing thing. "Uh, no, sir. I was, er, just surprised that we study Latin. That's all."

Teague clasped his hands behind his back. "And why is that, Luc? Do you think we are not civilized enough to handle such an ancient, honorable language?"

"No! That's not it at all. It was just because . . . well, no one studies Latin anymore. No one."

"They don't?" He sounded surprised.

"Well, nowhere I've ever heard of. It's pretty useless."

Teague frowned and huffed himself up. "It is the Lycanthian tradition to study the language of our ancestors. So in spite of your fascinating attempt at enlightenment, we will proceed. Unless you have anything else you'd like to add?" He glowered at me so threateningly that I quickly caught on that it was a rhetorical question.

By the time school let out at noon, I was pretty discouraged. My arms were full of books, and my stomach was empty. I thought about asking people what they did for lunch around here, then remembered I wasn't supposed to eat anything today. Which, of course, just made me all the more hungry.

I felt a shadow and looked up to see Nuri fall into step alongside me. "If you need any help with that science, let me know. That's the one subject I'm good at."

"Uh, thanks. I'm sure I'll need all the help I can get."

"You'll need to get somebody else to help you with Latin, though." He groped around in his pocket, searching for something. "I pretty much stink at that. Suki could do it, maybe. Or Killian." He finally produced a big wad of wrinkled-up, reddish-brown something and held it up triumphantly. "Want some jerky?" he asked.

One look at that piece of . . . flesh . . . and my appetite took a nosedive. "Uh, no thanks. I'm not supposed to eat anything today."

"Oh, yeah! I forgot." He clamped his teeth down on the jerky, ripping off a piece, then began to chew. "You nervous?"

I shrugged. Of course I was freaking nervous! I wasn't about to admit it, though.

Someone walked by off to my left, and I turned to see Rolfe and Wiley. "Hey, hobbler, see you tonight at your transformation," Wiley called out.

I turned to Nuri. "Hobbler?"

Nuri looked embarrassed. "'Cause you have to hobble around on only two legs." His face brightened. "But not for long!"

"Unless you get stuck partway through your change," Rolfe piped in.

Horrified, I stopped walking and turned to Nuri. "Stuck! What does he mean, stuck?"

Suki appeared at my side. "Don't worry, Luc. They're just trying to make you nervous. You won't get stuck. Not at our cairn."

Rolfe shrugged. "Still, it's a good thing you're so good at math, because you'll never be anything but half the wolf the rest of us are."

I shifted my books in my arms and started walking again.

"Yeah, you're nothing but a stupid half-breed," Wiley added.

I refused to let my irritation show. Guys like him just loved to know they were getting to you. "Well, isn't that the point? We're all half-breeds, half wolf and half human?"

Nuri snickered until Rolfe walked toward him, glaring.

Suki smiled at me. "Exactly."

"No. We're pure shifter, while he's half human, so he's less of a shifter than we are." Rolfe wouldn't let it go.

"So," I asked, ignoring him, "have all of you shifted already?"

There was a painful lull, like I had just asked some really stupid question and no one wanted to point it out to me. Suki bravely stepped forward.

"Well, really, it's only the half . . . er . . . shifters born of human mothers that don't shift until their thirteenth birthday. Those of us born to Lycanthian mothers can shift from the time we're first born," she explained.

I hated feeling stupid.

"But we can't control it on our own until we're thirteen," she hastened to add.

And I hated having so much to learn that I was probably going to feel stupid for the next five years. "So, are there any other half-breeds"—I realized I might as well get used to the term—"besides myself?"

"Well, there's Wanda," Risa said. "And Kevin. Have you met him yet? He was the tall one, sandy hair that falls into his face all the time?"

"Oh, yeah. I remember."

"And don't forget old Kora," Suki said. "She's half human as well."

"Yeah, and half useless." Rolfe smirked.

"Don't say that!" Suki said. "The older wolves deserve our respect, even if they can't hunt anymore. They have much they can teach us."

Wiley snorted. "Oh, give it up. They are useless. The only one lower in the pack is the Omega!"

"There is a place for everyone in the pack, Rolfe," Suki said. "All positions are important. Even the Omega."

"Yeah, you would say that. Come on, Wiley, let's get out of here." Rolfe turned. Before he'd taken two steps, he changed into his wolf form. A form I was just beginning to be able to recognize: a lanky wolf with brown fur that looked rough to the touch. He had four white socks and his brown tail was tipped with black. A second later, Wiley shifted and followed Rolfe into the nearby trees.

Risa sighed. "I pity any squirrels or chipmunks unlucky enough to cross their path."

Before I could ask any more questions, everyone began to walk away. I looked up and saw Ranger coming toward me. "Survived your first day of school?" he asked.

"Barely," I mumbled.

"Let's get rid of those books, then we'll head over to the cairn," he said, then led me back toward his house. He turned his head and peered down at me. "Well, how did it go?"

I shrugged as I pushed through the door into his living room. "It was okay." I dumped my books on a table, then turned to him. "Is it true that I might get stuck?" I blurted out.

"What?" His hand froze on the doorknob.

"Is it true that I might get stuck partway . . . partway between human and wolf?"

He crossed the room in three giant steps, grabbed my chin in his hands, and forced me to meet his eyes. "Who told you this?"

I jerked my chin out of his hands. "Rolfe. Is it true?"

He let me go and ran his hand over his head, then turned away from me and began pacing. This was not looking good.

"It is true that, *occasionally,* some half humans, half Lycanthians *can* get stuck. But only during specific circumstances. And those don't apply to you."

I settled my feet firmly on the ground and stared at him.

"What circumstances?" I wanted the whole truth and nothing but the truth. No more of these half answers.

"If you were to make your first change unaided by a pack, it is *slightly* possible that you might get stuck." He stopped pacing, crossed back to where I was standing, and put his hands on my shoulders. "But this will not happen to you, Luc. I promise."

I took a deep breath, relieved when something deep inside me untwisted. I hadn't realized just how much Rolfe's words had scared me. "Why does Rolfe hate me so much?" I asked.

He studied me for a minute before answering. "Doesn't that kind of thing happen in the human world? Aren't there certain people who like you and others who, for no particular reason, don't? We're not a utopia, merely a village of Lycanthians who struggle to make the best of their situation."

Ranger dropped his hands from my shoulders and went to look out the window. "The sad truth is, some of our pack members are highly suspicious of outsiders. Others are distrustful of any with human blood."

He turned to look at me, his eyes full of regret. "You, I'm afraid, are both."

We walked through the center of the village until we passed the last cabin and headed for the trees. "How far away is this cairn?" I asked.

Ranger shrugged. "Not far. Maybe ten minutes."

For the first time I realized just how big an area their village covered. "Do you guys own this land? Or just live out here hoping the forest service doesn't find out?"

He looked annoyed. "We . . . I . . . do not understand this concept you humans have of owning the land. The land simply is. If anything, it is we who belong to it. It gives us food and shelter and provides all the necessities we require, so how can we claim to own it?"

"It's just an expression," I said, lengthening my stride so I could keep up with him.

Ranger snorted. "Hardly. Humans have fought and died over land since the beginning of time, when clearly there can be enough for all. However, Lycanthians have learned the hard way to play by some of your rules. Many generations ago, when most of the land was still free and wild, some of our pack leaders claimed it as their own and exchanged the required gold for it."

"So, it *is* yours."

Ranger looked sharply at me. "No. Not ours. But we have purchased the right to use it, and to keep others from using it."

"Ho-kay."

After that, I shut up. The farther we walked on the narrow path, the more clustered the trees became. They grew taller and nearer together, a wall of rough bark and deep green. They seemed to encourage silence, like a church. The woods became thicker and thicker until I was certain we could go no farther, but then the path opened up and we stepped into a tiny clearing. Sasha was sitting on a boulder, waiting for us. The sun glinted off the white streak in her hair.

"Here we are then," Ranger said. "Has Teague arrived?"

"Yes." Sasha stood up. "He's gone ahead to the cairn." She turned her yellow cat's eyes toward me and smiled. "Come."

This path was so narrow I had to shove the branches aside so I could walk through. I wrestled with a particularly stubborn branch, finally stumbling past it into a large shady clearing.

Faint whispers of a thousand different voices rustled past my ears. As they whispered, something brushed across my skin, and it erupted into goose bumps. It felt like hundreds of cool, invisible cobwebs, all over my body. I shivered and tried to brush them away, but there was nothing there.

"What was that?" I asked.

Ranger stopped just behind me. "What was what?"

Sasha whirled around and cocked her head to the side. "You felt them?" she asked.

"I don't know who 'them' is, but I sure felt something." I rubbed my arms again, trying to chase away that invisible-cobweb sensation. The clearing was empty, but I had a strong sense of it being crowded with . . . something.

Sasha glanced quickly at Ranger, then back to me. "It's the spirits of the pack. Welcoming you, it seems." She folded her arms across her chest and studied me. "I can't decide which is more unusual: that you were able to feel them in human form, or that they welcomed you before your trans-formation. Well . . ." She smiled and reached out to tousle my hair. "They *have* been waiting for you for a long time."

I swallowed a little nugget of fear. "Why would spirits—or ghosts—be waiting for me?"

Sasha led me forward, and for the first time I noticed a large rock structure in the center of the clearing. It was four stacks of rocks, columns actually, with one enormous flat rock laid on top like a roof. It was tall, about as tall as Ranger, and the gray stone looked ancient.

"This is our cairn, and below it, our mundis. It is a very holy place for us," Sasha explained. "All of our dead are buried here. Every member of the pack has been buried here since we began."

Teague stepped out of the shadows and came toward us. "We have learned through hard experience that the closer to a cairn Lycanthians live, the more true to their heritage they are; their roots go deeper, their sense of pack unity is greater. Conversely, some Lycanths can pass with ease among humans and live nowhere near a cairn, but they are in much greater danger of turning rogue. They have no pack affiliation, no one to lend them strength or control, no spiritual connection."

"Can humans be buried here?" I asked, my eyes still on the cairn.

I felt rather than saw Teague and Sasha exchange glances. "Yes. If the pack agrees on it."

I cleared my throat. "Was my mother buried here?"

"Yes," Sasha said very gently. "Both your parents are buried here, and it is they who've been waiting for you for a very long time."

Sasha's words wrapped themselves around my heart. There was a quick jab of pain, then a sense of relief so strong it made my head spin. I reached out to gently touch the gray stone.

It screamed, and I jumped back. Sasha and Ranger looked at me, puzzled.

"Didn't you hear that?" I asked.

They looked at each other, and both said, "No."

Cautiously, I reached out and touched the stone again. Now that I was expecting it, I realized it wasn't so much a scream, as a loud rushing sound, like wind when it whips through the trees. Slowly, I took my hand away.

Teague took a few steps closer to us. "What did you hear, Luc?" The look on his face was intense; he seemed desperate to know what had happened, as if it mattered in some huge way I couldn't even guess at. Oddly, the more he wanted to know, the less I wanted to tell him. "N-nothing," I said.

Sasha stepped between Teague and me and put her arm around my shoulders. "The spirits of the pack live on forever. They never die or pass out of this world, but stay here, with us. They are our spirit guides, offering us protection and peace of mind. They lend us their strength and power in times of need. It is their strength, as well as ours, that will lend you control tonight as you make your first change."

"It is why you won't become stuck when you change," Ranger said. "You'll have not only your whole pack, but the spirits of hundreds of pack members lending you their power as you struggle with this new part of yourself."

"The cairn itself acts as a place where the division between the physical world and the spirit world is lessened," Sasha continued. "This way we stay close to the heart of the pack and the soul of the earth itself."

She turned and looked over at the cairn. "In some way that we don't understand, these rocks act almost like a sponge, and hold our pack's spiritual energy. If our village were discovered, and we had to leave, we could take the cairn stones with us, and the spirits of our ancestors would go with us as well.

"See here, Luc." She lifted a finger and touched one side of the cairn stones. I flinched, expecting to hear that scream again, and relaxed when I didn't. She narrowed her eyes slightly, and they seemed to glow a little more brightly. "Are you okay?"

"Yeah. I'm fine." *Just crazy*, I thought.

The area she pointed to was wavy and uneven, as if someone had taken a chisel to it. "Here is where we take the cairn chips and give them to Lycanthian children when they turn five years old. That's when they begin to control their own shapes separately from their parents. Full-blooded Lycanthians give those chips up at their thirteenth birthday, as a sign of their ability to shift without assistance. Half-blooded Lycanthians receive their cairn chip on their thirteenth birthday so they can use it as they learn their shape-shifting skills."

Well, the good news was, I'd have help. The bad news was, the help was a piece of rock.

Yeah, but it was a rock that screamed, I reminded myself.

15

When we got back to the cabin, Ranger heated up some stew for his dinner. I was glad I wasn't eating. My stomach had been taken over by butterflies the size of bats and didn't have any room left for something as ordinary as food.

Ranger seemed very relaxed as he ate. How could he be so calm at a time like this? I got up and began pacing. As I made my third pass by the table, Ranger looked down at my feet. "You'll have to get rid of those," he said, indicating my shoes.

"What?" I squawked. My Nikes were my pride and joy.

He sighed. "Nothing of man-made material can make the transformation with you—only those fabrics and materials found in nature. Cotton, wool, silk, leather. The power that transforms you is strong enough to transform the clothes and shoes you wear, as long as they are of the natural world. That means no polyester, no metal belt buckles, or shoe eyelets—nothing." He paused for a moment. "So," he said, impatience giving his voice a sharp edge, "unless you want those shoes to go *pouf* when you change, you will need to borrow a pair of my leather boots."

"Is that why you all wear such goofy clothes?" I asked, then immediately felt guilty.

Ranger raised an eyebrow at me. "Yes. And unless you want to wake up naked when you transform back to your human state, you will wear those goofy clothes as well."

"Works for me." If my choices were wearing goofy clothes, or ending up naked in a group full of strangers, I'd pick the goofy clothes any day. I hadn't realized there was a reason behind their outfits. I thought the Lycanthians here were just fashion-challenged.

Ranger got up from the table, cleared his plate, and went to his room to find me a pair of boots. When he came back, he tossed them at me and I caught them against my chest.

"Hurry," he said. "You don't want to be late for your first changing."

Says who? I thought. But I sat down and took off my Nikes, then shoved a foot into one of the boots. It was a little big, but it would do. Then I asked the question that had been bugging me ever since I'd heard that rock scream. "Will it hurt? Changing for the first time?"

Ranger cocked his head to the side and thought about that while I shoved my other foot into the boot. "No. Not hurt, exactly. But it isn't like anything you've ever felt before, and I don't know that you could actually call it a pleasant feeling."

Ranger opened the door for me and stood aside to let me go first. I started to walk through it, my heart lodged somewhere between my stomach and my throat. This was magic.

True magic, and it would change me . . . my life . . . forever. Was I ready for this? Did I really want this?

I stopped in the doorway and turned to him. "I don't have any choice in this, do I?"

Ranger looked at me with understanding eyes. "You always have a choice. Maybe not as to whether you change, but certainly a choice in how you do it. Whether you do it with pride and honor, or are dragged kicking and screaming, fighting the whole way."

Not sure if those last words were a threat, I stepped out into the night.

We quickly left the shelter of the village and passed into the wilderness just beyond the rough wooden buildings. As I passed under the trees, my skin could feel the roughness of the bark, and my tongue could taste the tangy sharpness of the sap, even though I touched neither.

We reached the cairn faster than I would have thought possible. Ranger's voice was soft in my ear. "Are you ready?"

I held back a nervous laugh. Was anyone ever really ready to see if they would turn into a werewolf? Even as I doubted with my mind and made fun of it with my words, my heart believed. My soul yearned with a longing I hadn't recognized until now. It seemed as if in some strange way, I'd been waiting for this my whole life.

"I'm as ready as I'll ever be," I told Ranger.

And with those words, I stepped into the clearing.

The moon was just rising over the mountains. It was as round and full as I'd ever seen it, and so bright it cast silvery light down onto the forest floor. The minute that silvery light touched my skin, something inside me began to lurch and boil as it scrambled to get closer to the moonlight. My skin hummed and my body knew, deep in its cells, that something was going to happen. Something that would change my life forever.

The whole pack was waiting, standing in a big circle around the cairn. Suki caught my eye and sent me an encouraging smile. Ulric stood next to Sasha. She wore a long gray robe with wide arms that fell back to her elbows. Her dark hair was loose, and the moonlight danced along the silver strands of it. Teague stood near them, watching me with eager, predatory eyes.

Then Ranger put his hand in the middle of my back and pushed me toward Sasha and Ulric.

As one, they stepped forward, took my hands, and led me closer to the cairn. Teague stepped toward us and began to speak, his deep voice flowing over the clearing.

"We welcome you into the pack, Luc, son of Kennet and Sara. The pack's strength is in its individuals, but your individual strength is tied directly to that of the pack. To diminish one is to diminish all. Honor your ties to your pack at all times. They come before all else."

At those words, Ulric and Sasha placed my hands on the columns of rock. As soon as my skin made contact, I could hear the screaming that wasn't really screaming. By the time Sasha and Ulric had stepped back, the sound had dulled to a rapid murmuring, as if hundreds of voices were all trying to speak at once, and none of them in a language I could understand.

I glanced around the circle of bodies that filled the clearing. The whole village was here, from the elders all the way down to the pups. A couple of them had already shifted to their wolf shapes. Ranger had warned me that some, especially the juveniles, hadn't yet achieved total command of their changing, and near the time of the full moon, they were apt to lose control.

Teague's voice continued. "Members of the pack never die; their spirit and power are part of us for all eternity." He reached forward and placed a leather cord around my neck. Dangling from the cord was a small piece of a cairn stone, glittering gray and white in the moonlight. As the stone fell into place against my throat, it felt warm. I felt the heat from the stone spread into me.

"You must honor the sacredness of this gift," Teague's voice continued. "We are guardians of the human race, not its enemies. The Lycanthian code forbids us to harm humans, except in extreme cases of self-defense. You must honor this law or be cast from the pack to roam as a rogue wolf forever."

At the word *forever*, I gasped. The chip of rock burned, and I had the sensation of a hundred different breezes rushing through me, lifting me. My body began to swirl, as if my skin had turned into thousands of little pinwheels. I glanced up, not surprised to see that the moon had cleared the mountaintops. It hung in the sky in all its glimmering white glory, a primitive force that spoke directly to my blood.

As my skin shimmied and swirled, trying to dance its way off my body, my blood began to flow faster, hotter. I was aware of it coursing through my veins, pumping through my heart. It was like a living thing inside me, trying to writhe its way out.

I glanced up at Sasha and Ulric, who watched me with kindness in their eyes and welcome in their hearts. I could feel this welcome, like a ray of sun, shining from them. I wanted to run and roll myself in the scent of their acceptance.

Before I could think about this, a wrenching sensation ripped through me. It wasn't pain, not quite, but a stretching and shifting of muscles, bone, and sinew into a shape they'd never been in before. Panting now, I looked down at my hands, gaping as the fingers grew shorter before my eyes, the fingernails thickening, lengthening into claws.

My ears popped, and suddenly I could hear everything. I could hear the breeze whispering to the trees. I heard the heartbeats of the pack as they stood in the circle, the sound of their bodies changing just like mine was.

I could hear the moon moving through the sky.

The crawling sensation on my skin grew more urgent. Even as I watched, small hairs began to spring out of my skin, so fast and so thick that it was like watching grass growing in fast motion.

I became so dizzy I could barely stand. It was as if everything inside me, every one of my internal organs, had decided to do somersaults and cartwheels, backflips and loop-the-loops. Unable to stand any longer, I dropped to all fours, jolted out of my fog long enough to realize I didn't have to bend my knees. I was on all fours, and it felt right, comfortable. A huge rush of energy filled me . . . joy, strength. I wanted to run. More than anything I found myself wanting to give in to this urge and run through the forest. A need rose up in my throat. I wanted to shout this joy up to the treetops, all the way to the moon.

In front of me, Ulric was now an enormous timber wolf, his fierce, proud eyes glowing in the moonlight. He lifted his head and howled, an achingly joyous sound full of welcome.

Next Sasha picked up the howl, then Ranger and Sterling and all the rest. I stood surrounded by wolves of every shape and color, their heads thrown back to the moon as they howled, welcoming me.

Then I, too, lifted my voice in that primal song and proclaimed to the moon, to everyone, that I had come home.

16

Then I ran. I couldn't help it. I could no more have stood still than I could have turned back into my human form.

My wolf body leaped away from the cairn, and I found myself nimbly picking my way out of the clearing. When I reached the trees, I gave in to the urge to go full speed. My muscles flexed and rippled. I could feel the air streaming past as I ran faster than I could have imagined. Faster, it seemed, than the very wind itself.

The entire pack followed me, streaming behind like the tail of a comet.

You would think with a new body I would have stumbled or felt awkward, but I didn't. I was a streamlined projectile racing through the forest on silent feet, my body a well-oiled machine, pumping with power and speed. I could not be stopped. It felt like I had been waiting for this my whole life. My feet—paws—barely touched the ground as I sprang from forest floor to fallen log to tumbling rocks.

And it wasn't only my speed that was different. I didn't just run through the woods, I absorbed them through my very pores until I could hardly tell where I ended and the forest began. We were one.

The forest floor was a carpet of decaying leaves, pine needles, and a rich loamy earth that smelled of wild things, growing and hidden. It was such a strong rich scent, it made my nose twitch, and I sneezed, the sound cracking through the silence like gunshot. On this rock I could smell where a squirrel had been minutes ago, and that he'd been afraid. Over on the fallen log, I smelled raccoon, a male who had been washing a small fish he'd caught. The woods were like a book that only my nose knew how to read. I went over to the stream, bent my head to the water, and drank deeply. It was cold and clear, and tasted like moonlight.

I felt a tug on my tail and turned to find my grandfather behind me, his tongue lolling out in a big wolfish grin. He reached out with jaws that could crush a moose's foreleg and gently snagged my tail between his teeth. He tugged again, then turned and ran away, watching over his shoulder to make sure I'd follow. I never thought twice; I just turned and chased after him.

Soon, Suki and Nuri joined us, and it was an odd combination of tag, chase, and tail tug-of-war.

I was amazed at how much I was able to understand. My wolf mind knew all sorts of ways to communicate without words: barks and howls, throaty whines, short growls, and clicks. And that wasn't even counting our ears and tails. There were hundreds of ways to move them, each meaning something different.

Out of the corner of my eye I saw a small furry creature

scurry out from under a boulder into the moonlight. A mouse! Before my mind had registered more than that, my body pounced. When I looked down, I'd managed to snare its tail under my paw. My other paw came down on the far side of it, trapping it between my forelegs. It jumped, nearly landing on my nose, and I reared back in surprise, letting go of the tail. The little fellow scampered off a few feet, and I moved in again, pounced, and missed.

It was a quick little sucker and darted to the left. Pounce. Miss. Then it darted to the right. Pounce. Pawful of pine needles, but no mouse. I looked around just in time to see the tip of a tail disappear down a hole in the ground.

A low noise in the trees off to my left caught my attention. I flattened to my belly and crept closer. There was another rustle and chirp. A raccoon leaped out in front of me, making a mad dash for cover. I was so startled, I just stood there and watched it run away and scurry into a small, hollowed-out log.

I heard a twig snap behind me and turned to find Rolfe and Wiley slinking toward me. Rolfe's head was lowered and his ears back. He stared, his eyes never leaving mine as he kept moving forward.

My whole body went on alert. I had enough instinct to tell me this was an aggressive challenge, but not enough to know why. Had I broken some sacred wolf rule? Or did he just not like me?

I stared back and bared my teeth. A low growl began somewhere in my chest. Wiley hung back and Rolfe stepped forward, slowly circling me. I hunched my shoulders, reassured by the powerful muscle rippling at my command. I showed more teeth, growled even louder.

Rolfe feinted toward me, swiping his front paw in my direction. It was only intended to draw me out, to force me to make the first move. I ignored the taunt and hunkered down, ready to spring at the first opening he gave me.

Why was he doing this? Why couldn't he just leave me alone?

With a start, I realized I could make this go away. Somehow, deep in my bones, I knew how. All I had to do was look down, hang my head, and get low to the ground. Show him I was submissive. Let him dominate. But my muscles and brain refused. They whispered of strength and speed, power and instinct. The need to stand my ground. My birthright.

I leaped, lunging teeth first toward Rolfe's neck. I saw his eyes widen in surprise, then we were locked together, rolling on the ground. Deep harsh sounds sprang from my throat. Sounds of protest. Sounds of anger. A deep growl that let him know that I would not lie still for this. Not now. Not ever again. Today, I had been given the power and the strength, and I was going to use it.

At the last minute, Rolfe twisted to the left and my teeth landed on his shoulder. He reached around with his muzzle and nipped at my ear.

Round and round we rolled, a confused heap of legs, fur, and teeth all scrambling for position and opportunity. First I'd gain the advantage, then he would. No sooner would I be sure I had his body under me than he'd twist like a piece of coiled steel and slip out of my grasp.

Slowly, I became aware of other wolves gathering around us.

With one final twist of my body, I rolled on top of Rolfe

and buried my teeth in the soft fur of his neck. I could feel Rolfe's blood, his life's energy pulsing furiously beneath my tongue. With one sharp press of my teeth, I could destroy it. Him.

That thought filled me, my veins practically bursting with the thought of such power, mine for the taking. But it wasn't time. It was only time to show Rolfe that we were equals, and I had done that.

I stepped back from Rolfe's prone body, slowly, savoring the vision of him lying on the ground, belly up, neck exposed, totally submissive to me.

Finally, I was free of the burdens of being small. Of being a shrimpy little wuss. I was my own master. No one could tell me what to do, or I'd bite their stupid head off. I was so full of my own power and magnificence that I threw back my head and howled, letting all that energy flow out of me into the night.

Before I could finish gloating over the submissive Rolfe, Ranger and Ulric appeared at our sides. With a growl and a snap, Ulric's huge gray form hurtled toward me, made contact, and sent me tumbling to the forest floor. From that point on, my body took over and my mind just sat back and watched in fear. There was a loud, snarling growl just two inches from my face. I pressed my back flat against the ground, my eyes rolled up until the white part showed, and I was careful not to meet Ulric's furious gaze in case he saw that as a further challenge. He buried his teeth in my neck, and I froze. Part of me feared he was going to rip out my throat, but another part somehow knew that he wouldn't. He used his jaws to shake the spit out of me, my head clunking back and forth.

It was irritating how easily my body cowered before him, almost as if my mind didn't have any control over it. Only when I was completely submissive and Ulric was certain I wasn't going to give him any more trouble did he get off me. He did it slowly, staring at me the whole time as if to make sure I wasn't going to try anything stupid.

He didn't need to worry. I wasn't.

When he was all the way off, he sat back on his haunches and waited for Ranger to finish giving Rolfe his wolf scolding. I rolled on my side to watch, too.

Finally, Ranger gave one last shake to Rolfe's throat, then pulled away. He turned from Rolfe's submissive body, and trotted over to where I lay. Nudging me with his nose, he checked to see how I'd fared, then coaxed me to a sitting position. As I sat up, my brains felt scrambled from Ulric's punishment, and I found myself wondering if beating the crap out of Rolfe had been worth it.

Oh, yeah. It had.

Just as the moon disappeared over the horizon, another howl went up: Ulric calling the pack in to settle down for the night. I howled back to let him know I was coming and trotted in the direction the sound had come from. I couldn't help but wonder if Rolfe would hold a grudge.

Within minutes, the whole pack had gathered around Ulric. When he flopped to the ground with a tired grunt, we all did the same. Soon we were nothing but a big pile of fur—gray, white, brown, and black. As I nestled in among the pack, I felt an incredible peace come over me, as if I had finally answered some question that had been plaguing me ever since I could remember. All around me I could feel the power of the pack. I don't just mean its strength, but its energy. I could sense the different threads of individual wolves' power just like the different threads in a tangled knot. Ulric's power was the greatest, firm and strong, uncomplicated. It spoke of protection and justice. Right under his I could sense Ranger's. His had a whiff of danger to it, and a little more humor. Nuri's was mischievous, Suki's loyal and sincere, Luna's patient and all-forgiving. I found I could locate everyone in the pack just by focusing on their thread of power that hung in the air.

After a few minutes of concentrating, I noticed there were other strains of power, but none that I recognized. They weren't attached to a specific wolf, just the pack. I picked my way through these other threads, shocked when one I touched tasted of my father. Of my memories of him. It tasted of strength, but equally of caring. I wrapped that strand of power around myself and gently drifted off to sleep.

17

I woke up when a bright ray of sunlight fell across my eyelids. When I turned away from the sun and tried to snuggle back into sleep, I bumped into something solid and warm.

I opened my eyes to see what it was, nearly yelping in shock when I found myself in the middle of a heap of bodies. Human bodies. I froze and slammed my eyes shut. The last thing I remembered was the entire pack collapsing on the forest floor in one exhausted, contented heap. That was it. We must have all returned to our human forms while we slept.

Someone's leg was thrown over mine. An arm was flung across my chest. I had no idea whose arm it was, and I didn't really want to know. Right about then, I realized that my head was resting on *some* part of someone for a pillow. I started to jerk away, then froze as someone muttered something in their sleep.

Why did I have to be the first one to wake up?

I stared up at the branches overhead. When I was in wolf form, it felt perfectly normal to pile up with a bunch of other wolves and fall asleep. Now it just felt totally weird.

Just thinking of being in my wolf body made me smile. Last night, instead of backing down or trying to find a peaceful solution, I'd fought tooth and claw against Rolfe. And enjoyed it. I had loved feeling my powerful muscles slam into his body, meet resistance, and push through to victory. I had taken pleasure in forcing him to the ground, insisting he acknowledge that I was the winner. Me, not him. Oh, if Joey could see me now. Or Coach Grimshaw.

Or Uncle Stephen.

At the thought of Uncle Stephen, something fluttered deep inside. What would he have thought about that fight last night? What would he have done if he'd seen me in the shape of a wolf? He would have called me an abomination, like my father. Now that I knew what it meant, did I care?

Whoever my head was resting on picked that moment to stir. Their slight movement let me move my head off the leg I'd been using as a pillow. Feeling self-conscious, I allowed my gaze to follow the leg upward. It was Luna's.

Hot prickly embarrassment rushed through me. I sat up quickly, not caring who I woke up. I'm sorry, but you just don't go around using other people's legs as pillows. Especially people you don't know very well. And especially girls who your uncle might have a thing for. Sheesh. Major awkward moment.

I turned to look back at Luna, hoping she'd still be asleep. Her pale silver eyes were open, and she smiled at me. "'Morning, Luc."

Still embarrassed, I dropped my gaze. "'Morning," I mumbled.

Even though my cheeks burned with embarrassment, her casual acceptance of all this made it a little easier for me to stomach. A little, but not much. I still wanted to be any-where but here, curled up in a pile of strangers' bodies.

No, a voice inside my head rang out, *not strangers. Family. Pack. Yours.* A little of the tightness in my stomach began to go away.

Just then, there was a thump on my back. "Relax," Ranger said. "You're wearing your discomfort like a cheap coat."

"Uncomfortable? Who says I'm uncomfortable?" I turned and let my eyes move over the whole crowd of bod-ies, proving to him they didn't bother me a bit. Of course I was careful not to let my eyes actually *focus* on anything.

"Let's go find some breakfast." His mouth still twitched in amusement.

Have I mentioned how much I hate it when people think I'm funny and I'm not trying to be?

When I got to the kitchen, Ranger was just spooning scram-bled eggs out of a frying pan onto two plates. The table was already set with forks and two glasses of orange juice.

"Aha," I said. "So you do eat something besides meat."

"Occasionally, yes."

We both sat down to breakfast, and all of a sudden my hunger reached up and pinched me. I was starving! Chang-ing physical shape took a lot out of a person. I picked up my fork and dug into my eggs.

Ranger ate his breakfast more slowly. Slow enough so he

could talk in between bites. "After school today, the juveniles will show you around some more. They'll explain what their daily duties are, what they do for recreation, that sort of thing. I'm sure they'll make you feel right at home."

Personally, I had my doubts, but before I could tell him, there was a knock at the door. Ranger got up to open it. My nose picked up the scent of nervousness, concern, and anxiety.

"Remus! What brings you here?" Ranger threw a glance at me over his shoulder, then stepped out onto the front porch, closing the door behind him.

As hard as I strained, I couldn't make out a single word they said. A few minutes later, when Ranger came back in, his face was grim.

"Who was it?" I asked as I cleared my plate.

"The Fenriki from the Mabon Pack. I need to take him to Ulric." He didn't sit back down, but instead grabbed his plate and tossed the rest of the eggs into the trash. Tension and anger rolled off him in waves.

"What's wrong?" I asked, my voice sounding small and scared, even to my ears.

His eyes flashed hard and angry. "Nothing we can't handle this time."

"This," Teague said, tapping the pointer at the wolf skull, "is our jaw. A vital part of our wolf selves. We can exert an amazing amount of pressure, up to fifteen hundred pounds. Which is twice as much as a dog, I might add." He said the last part with a great deal of pride. "While our jaws were designed for snapping moose bones in two, they are also used for carrying, communicating, and reprimanding. We must never forget that it is one of our most deadly weapons, and must be used carefully. Now, let's go outside so you can test this for yourselves."

We stood up and headed outside. As we crowded against the door waiting to get out, I somehow managed to get shoved up against Rolfe. I braced myself for something ugly, some mention of last night, but he just glared at me, then slunk out the door with Wiley tagging along behind him like one of Little Bo-Peep's sheep.

Being a werewolf definitely had its advantages.

I tried not to swagger as I walked out of the schoolroom, but it was hard. Knowing I'd never have to be meek and passive again made me want to throw my head back and howl with glee. Funny thing is, I didn't realize I was being a doormat before. I thought it was just my personality. Boy, was I wrong.

Once we were all outside, Teague called out, "Now change, please." My newfound confidence scattered. I didn't have a clue how to change on my own. Talk about two giant steps backward! Sure, I'd changed last night, but I had no idea *how*.

My cheeks burned with humiliation at the thought of letting Teague—not to mention Rolfe—know I was helpless when it came to changing on my own. And just how long would it take Rolfe to start dishing out crap again, once he realized I couldn't change at will? I fingered the cairn chip I'd been given at my Transformation Ceremony.

I looked up to find Rolfe sneering at me, almost as if he were reading my thoughts.

Someone touched my elbow, and I turned to find Suki

standing beside me, her silver-green eyes full of understanding. "Do you need help changing?" She kept her voice low.

"Uh, yeah. Can you help me?"

"No problem." She turned and called out to Nuri.

Nuri turned around. "Huh?"

Suki jerked her head in my direction.

"Oh. Gotcha. Be right there." He came over and stood next to us.

"Just close your eyes, Luc," Suki said. "And try to relax."

I closed my eyes and immediately felt Nuri's power, a bristly erratic thread, knocking and bumping against me, trying to get in. A second later, Suki's power, smoother and cooler, wrapped itself around Nuri's and focused the energy. It paused for a moment, then pushed through. The two threads of power stumbled around inside me, fumbling and groping as if they were trying to get their arms around a rock that was much too big for them. Finally, after a lot of confusion that made me very dizzy, I felt a great push, like I was being squeezed from the inside out, then a big pop, and I felt my own power begin to flow out and around me.

The change had begun. The almost-but-not-quite pain of my bones stretching, my muscles lengthening, a furious prickling bringing my fur up to the surface. Then I dropped to all fours and spent a moment trying to orient myself.

I loved being in my wolf form. I wanted to run and jump and smell the thousand different smells that teased my nose, but Teague called us to him. Three piles of branches lay next to him on the ground.

"Let's begin, class," Teague said. Then he tossed each one of us a stick from one of the piles.

Once we all had one, he said, "Now, bite down on the stick, paying careful attention to how much force you exert until you hear the wood cracking."

The first thing I noticed was, when you have your mouth wrapped around something, a lot of drool tends to run out the side of your mouth. I tried to slurp it back in, but didn't really know how to make my wolf mouth do that particular trick. So there I sat with a stick in my mouth and drool running down my chin. Total wolf moment.

Then I pressed my sharp teeth down into the soft wood until the branch cracked, then began to break apart. Suddenly I was standing there with a mouth full of splinters. It was a lot like having popcorn hulls stuck in your teeth, only pokier.

"Second branch, same thing," Teague called out. These second branches were much thicker, so he came around and laid one down in front of each of us.

Except I ran into a small problem. Picking up a stick is a lot harder than you'd think. Before you can get your teeth around it, your nose gets a snoutful of dirt because it's smashed up against the ground. I looked around to see how others were doing it. They all seemed to have a better technique than I did, one that involved sort of pushing their teeth out of their mouth, or maybe they were pulling their lips back, I couldn't tell.

After about ten tries, I finally got it.

"Third branch," Teague called out as he walked around and put another, even thicker one in front of us. These were about as thick as a man's leg. "Again," he said, "pay attention to the amount of force you exert."

I bent my muzzle to the ground and picked up the branch. I wrapped my teeth around it and pressed down. Could my jaw really break a branch this thick? Down, down, down, my teeth sank into the wood. The branch pressed up into my gums, smashing up into the sides of my face. Without warning, the stick snapped. One end of it went spinning through the air. I watched as it spun, wondering where it was going to land, then yelped when a hand reached up and snagged it out of the air.

Ranger. I hadn't noticed him approaching. I quickly lifted my lips off my teeth in a nervous, apologetic grin.

"Good morning, Ranger," Teague said. "What brings you out here?"

"I've some news I'd like to share with the class when you're done here."

"Your timing is perfect. We've just finished." Teague turned from Ranger to us. "Let's return to the classroom now."

Little eddies of energy swirled all around me in the clearing, and in place of wolves, there were now eight kids. Except for me. I stood there without a clue how to change back into my human shape. Ranger strolled over to me.

"Can you turn back into your human shape by yourself yet?" he asked.

I shook my head. Some big, powerful werewolf I was. I'd ended up asking for help more often in the last twenty-four hours than I ever had in my old life.

Ranger reached out and gently placed his hand across my eyes, touching at each of my temples. "Picture yourself in human form, Luc. Envision your legs, your arms, your whole body, then finally your head," he said softly.

I closed my eyes and did what he said, slowly imagining the whole shifting process, but in reverse. Nothing happened. Then Ranger rubbed gently at my temples and muttered a word under his breath. As if in slow motion, I could feel my humanness being pulled up from some place within me. It oozed upward and outward, struggling slightly and wiggling a bit. I felt a flash and a swirl and a pop, like the very essence of me had just been yanked from my body.

"Th-thanks," I managed, then followed Ranger into the classroom and took my seat. He continued on to the front of the class, where he perched himself on the edge of Teague's desk.

"The Fenriki from the Mabon Pack came to our village this morning," he explained. "The Mabon are closer to the city than we are, and they wanted to give us a warning."

He stopped talking and drew a deep breath, as if he were uncertain as to how to continue.

"For the most part, we are safe here in our village. But every once in a while, danger finds us. The Mabon wanted to warn us that abolitionist execution squads have been spotted in the area."

Everyone fell silent, and fear began to creep into the room.

Slowly, I raised a hand. I was embarrassed to have to ask, but everyone's fear made me realize it was important, too important to ignore. "What's an abolitionist?"

Teague's eyes and voice were hard. "Abolitionists are those who feel that Lycanthians are evil and must be stamped out. By whatever means necessary. Including murder. They will stop at nothing to destroy every last one of us."

That stopped me cold. There were people out there who hated us. Me. They were willing to kill us, just for being Lycanthians. "Can't you—we—go to the police? Won't they offer us protection?"

Ranger barked out a sharp, bitter laugh. "Lycanths are not accepted by the general public, Luc. In fact most people assume we are a myth, a legend. But there is a very passionate minority who think we are an abomination."

Abomination. There was that word again.

Rolfe raised his hand. "Why now?" he asked, throwing me one of his I-wish-you-would-just-die looks.

Ranger shifted his weight on the desk and ignored Rolfe's question. "The Mabon wanted us to be aware of the problem and be extra alert during the next few weeks. This means we will increase perimeter patrols and double the checkpoint duty. It also means we will have to postpone your field trip to the city that was scheduled for next week."

This announcement was met by a huge chorus of groans and boos until Ranger held up a hand, and everyone fell quiet. "Your safety is not negotiable. These increases in activity seem to go in cycles, and once this cycle has run its course, we'll reschedule the trip."

18

Hours later, Teague called out, "Class dismissed. And don't forget: You gather at the north end of the village before dawn for the hunt."

There was a lot of snapping and shuffling as books were closed and papers hastily tucked back into desks. Nuri was the first one out of his seat. I stood up, eager to follow. Before I could get very far, Rolfe walked by my desk and bumped into me, sending me tumbling back into my chair. "Are you happy now that you've put us all in danger?"

"What are you talk—"

"Enough!" growled Teague, descending on Rolfe as if he intended to rip his throat out. Instead, he pointed toward the door and snarled, "You're dismissed."

"Not you," Teague told Nuri as he tried to sneak by. "As per Ulric's orders, you're staying in to review pack protocol."

Nuri groaned, then schlepped back to his desk. I was halfway out of my seat again when Teague said, "You, too,

Luc. This will be an excellent opportunity for you to begin learning our ways."

Rats. I lowered myself back down. Detention already.

"Up front, please," Teague said, and rapped his pointer on one of the front desks.

Nuri and I got up and moved to the front row. Teague leaned against his desk, folded his arms across his chest, and looked down at Nuri.

"Nuri, for review; what is Ulric's position within the pack?"

"Alpha."

"And what does being Alpha mean?"

"It means that he is the first among us."

Teague glared at Nuri. "Would you please tell us what that means?"

I think Nuri squirmed under Teague's gaze, but it was hard to tell with all his regular twitching and fidgeting.

"The Alpha rules the pack, and it's through his wishes that we do all things."

I turned to look at Teague. Surely this couldn't be right. But he just nodded and said, "Can you eat without his permission?"

"No."

"Can you hunt large game, leave the village, or speak to those who aren't pack members without his permission?"

Here Nuri sighed. "No."

"Exactly. And what is your position in the pack?"

"A juvenile."

"And what is the juvenile's standing in the pack?"

Nuri looked down at the desk and picked at a hangnail. "At the very bottom, just before the Omega."

"So technically, you owe obedience to everyone above you, yes?"

Nuri nodded.

"Everyone in the pack except other juveniles and the Omega has authority over you. Remember that, and just be glad they don't overuse the privilege."

"Yes, sir," Nuri mumbled to his hangnail.

Teague turned that piercing gaze of his to me, and I flinched. "Do you have something to say?"

"Does Ulric's authority over us take priority over our parents' or guardian's?" I asked.

"Excellent question. And yes, it does, but it rarely comes to that," Teague explained.

"And how old do we have to be before this total authority over us ends?" I asked.

Teague stared at me in surprise. "Why . . . never. Ulric has authority over all the pack members, adults included. If not we would have . . . anarchy."

"If not," I said without thinking, "you would have democracy."

"You," he said, taking a step forward and towering over me, "of all people, owe us your absolute, blind obedience." He stared at me for a minute, as if he would have liked to say more, then turned back to Nuri. "Especially now," he said, lifting his head to stare out the window. "With danger drawing closer, it is critical that we maintain pack discipline." He was quiet for a moment before speaking again. "Now go. Oh, and Nuri. I'm sorry, but Ulric has decided you are not to go on the hunt tomorrow."

Nuri's face fell. His disappointment was so thick it tickled the back of *my* throat.

"He needs to know you can be trusted to know your place," Teague continued. "The hunt is too dangerous to risk any unreliability. You're to report to the nursery for your chores this afternoon."

Nuri stood and shuffled in a very un-Nuri-like way to the door. I followed him, but as soon as we were outside, I turned and pounced. "What did he mean by that? That I of all people owed them blind obedience?"

He shook his head, looking positively miserable, and wouldn't meet my eyes. I didn't know how far to push him. I mean, we'd only been friends a couple of days. And it wasn't like there were people lining up to take his place. I decided I'd let it go for now, but I'd start paying much closer attention in the future. Something was definitely going on, and everyone seemed to be trying to hide it from me.

We made our way to one of the cabins at the southeast end of town. Instead of going up to the front door, Nuri led me around the back to a huge yard. At first, I saw nothing, then with a yip and a yap, three little wolf pups came romping our way, tripping over their own and one another's feet before they reached us. Suki trailed behind.

They were so cute! They wriggled around at my feet, sniffing my boots. A little black one grabbed my pant leg and began tugging me back toward the trees. His sturdy front legs scrabbled in the dirt as he tried to drag a hundred pounds clenched between his sharp little teeth. Before I could stop him, I heard a loud rip, then he was tumbling backward through the grass until he landed on his butt in surprise. I burst out laughing, which seemed to startle him.

"Oh, good. New victims." Suki brushed her hair out of her face. She looked tired. "The one that's feasting on your pant leg is Keir, a fearless pup that I spend much of my time watching."

Nuri bent down and snatched up a small medium-gray ball of fluff. It had green eyes and kept trying to lick his chin as if it were covered in honey. Or whatever it is that wolf pups find tasty. It could be deer heart, for all I knew. "Who's got who now, Kana? Huh?" Nuri teased the small pup as he wrestled with it and tickled it. Kana got very excited—too excited. Nuri jumped back two feet and held out the pup at arm's length while she peed.

"I was just going to ask if I could hold one, but I think I've changed my mind," I said.

"Oh, don't worry. Just don't tickle them to death and you'll do fine," Suki said drily. "This little one here trying to eat your boot is Zola," she said, looking down at yet another pup.

I reached down and picked up Zola. She was a lot heavier than she looked, and she wriggled something fierce. She sniffed my face first, then my hands, trying to crawl onto my shoulder.

"Watch the teeth," Suki said just as I snatched my hand away from the nipping little jaw.

"Can they change yet?" I asked. "I mean, do they have a human shape, too?"

"Yes, but they can't control it. They usually take whatever shape their parents are in."

I put Zola back on the ground, and she immediately

bounded over to Keir and began tugging at the scrap of pant leg. Thirty seconds later, they were off in a game of tag.

"Come on," Suki said. "If we don't hurry, we'll never catch them."

After I'd been chewed on, tugged on, and peed on, I was ready for a break.

I heard a whisper of sound, and an adult gray wolf emerged from the trees behind the house. There was a swirl in the air, then a woman stood where the wolf had been. Suki nodded to the woman as she approached us. "That's Rhea," Suki said. "She's Zola's mother. It was her day to watch the pups, but all the adults have been called to help with perimeter patrol today."

As Rhea walked toward us, she looked tired, and there were lines of worry etched around her eyes.

Seeing her mother approach, Zola became even more wiggly and wanted to be put down. I placed her on the ground, and she was off like a rocket through the tall grasses toward her mother, where she yipped and nipped at her heels.

After a couple of nips, Zola stopped moving and kept very still, grunting a bit. Kind of like when little kids are doing something dirty in their diaper. A quick swirl of color, and there was a curly-headed toddler with her thumb stuck firmly in her mouth. Rhea reached down and picked up Zola, then hugged her close to her body, burying her face in the toddler's hair.

Suki was immediately concerned. "Is everything okay?"

Rhea lifted her face and laid her cheek on Zola's head. "So far. We have learned nothing more, if that is what you mean. But it's so unsettling." She shivered a little. "It reminds me of . . . before." She glanced quickly at me then looked away.

There it was again. The sense of unspoken things lurking just beneath the surface, and I hated it.

19

Just before dawn the next morning, a small group of us gathered at the south end of the village. Everyone seemed excited, like athletes before a big game. When Niall, the Beta, appeared, a hush fell over the group and the excitement fell away, leaving a sense of purpose and discipline hanging in the cool air.

Niall was a big man, nearly as tall as Ulric, but less bulky, a little more lanky. He stopped in front of Ranger and frowned. "I still think he's too new to go on his first hunt."

Ranger shook his head in disagreement. "Ulric and I both agree that he needs to learn everything he can as quickly as possible. Who knows how soon he'll need to rely on his hunting skills."

A silent look passed between the two of them, then Niall sighed and looked at me. "Very well. But there are a couple of things you must understand before we leave. You will be an observer only. You will not—must not—participate. The hunt can be extremely dangerous. I don't want you gored by an antler or slashed by a sharp hoof before you even know what you're doing."

Made perfect sense to me. "Yes, sir."

His mouth turned up at the corners in an attempt to smile. "In order to help you learn as much as possible, I've invited Sterling along. Normally, he would be considered too old to participate, although he would—and does—argue that point with me often. However, today I'm making an exception."

My grandfather was coming! Perfect. "Thank you, sir."

Niall turned to Ranger. "I'll need you up front."

Ranger slapped me on the shoulder. "See you at the end," he said, then followed Niall to the front of the crowd. As they passed, people began to change into their wolf forms.

I clutched my cairn chip and tried not to feel out of place.

As I wondered what to do, I saw Sterling coming my way. There was a bounce in his step and a twinkle in his eye. Just seeing him like that put me in a good mood.

He gave me a big hug, then pulled back to look me in the eyes. "Looking forward to your first hunt?" he asked.

"Uh. Not really. Hunting isn't real popular back where I come from."

"I know. Kennet explained it to me once." I waited for the familiar sadness to cloud his eyes at the mention of my father, but it didn't. "Any questions?" he asked.

"Not really. Ranger already explained to me why we don't go to the store and buy hamburger."

He threw back his head and laughed. "Oh, Luc. Only humans deserve to eat something as stupid as cows." After he'd finished laughing, he continued with his explanation.

"No, the food we take is sacred, a covenant between us and the prey who wish to die."

"Wait a minute," I said. "*Wish* to die?"

Sterling's eyes grew sharp. "Oh, yes. Make no mistake. There is always a choice. It takes two, the predator and the prey, to decide when the dance will end in death." He glanced up and saw the group beginning to gather behind Niall. "So," he said. "It is time. Do you need help shifting?"

Embarrassed, I shrugged. "I don't know. Probably. I always have so far."

Sterling smiled. "Don't look so glum. Most Lycanthians go through years of assisted changes before they can do it on their own. Begin, and I will help you."

I nodded, feeling hideously self-conscious, like I was about to get naked in public. I grasped my chip in one hand and closed my eyes.

With only a gentle flutter of warning, I felt Sterling's power reach out and tap against mine until it broke the surface like the shell of an egg. His power surged inside briefly, winding itself around my wolf and leading it out. It was so different from the way Nuri and Suki had helped me. With them, it was like being shoved through a hole in a fence that was too small. With Sterling, it was more like he forged a crack that I was able to find my way through.

I couldn't tell if the physical changing was becoming less painful, or if I was just more used to it. Either way, as my bones stretched and my muscles expanded, it felt a little more familiar and a lot less disturbing.

Niall's opening howl called to us. Sterling and I were ready and howled back our signal. Then we were off: one long, silent string of wolves in search of food.

We trotted for miles, the wolves at the front stopping often to sniff a hoofprint here, a pile of scat there. I had no idea what they were looking for, but I didn't care. Trotting through the woods as dawn broke was enough for me. The fresh air against my fur, the smells of the whole world waking up; I was happy.

As we followed the pack, Sterling had me stop and smell everything that the leaders had examined. No sooner did I sniff than a picture of the creature would form in my mind. I had my first scent of deer, a big aggressive buck, a young female, and a yearling who was still nervous. I smelled rabbit and raccoon, and got a big whiff of elk that made my eyes water.

Up in front, Niall stopped and took his time smelling something, then called Ranger over for a second opinion. Next, Niall called three wolves from the front of the pack. I recognized Killian, but not the other two, although I could tell they were female by their narrower chests and slightly shorter legs.

The five in the front fanned out, swiftly and silently. A heightened sense of anticipation fell over the rest of us, and we followed through the trees, but from a distance.

Sterling motioned for me to follow him. Suki, who had been trotting next to me, began to fall back, until he motioned for her to join us as well. Sterling led us to the front and off to the side so we could see what was happening.

I heard the sounds of many hooved feet pawing the ground, of flat large teeth quietly grinding grass. I could smell deer, lots and lots of deer. My heart began to race.

We crept forward, inching closer to our quarry. I could see them now, a small herd of about fifteen deer, grazing.

The breeze rustled through my fur, shifting slightly. A big buck with four pronged antlers lifted his head. On alert now, all the deer lifted their heads. In a flash, they turned tail and bounded away. We were left staring at an empty meadow. The lead wolves turned from the clearing to search for a new scent.

We continued the hunt in silence until Niall froze. Following his lead, we all stopped in our tracks, and only then did we see the enormous moose he'd stumbled upon.

Niall's eyes were intense as they focused on the moose, almost as if they were asking some vital question. The moose calmly lifted its enormous head and stared back at Niall with steady eyes, almost daring him to try something. After as good a staring contest as I've ever seen, the moose turned from Niall and walked away, flicking his tail in disdain. Niall stood for a minute and watched the moose. I half expected him to start chasing it or something, but he didn't. He just let it walk away.

A sense of grim determination settled over the pack.

Not long after that, the front wolves picked up a scent again. Another small conference took place, only this time, when they moved out, they peeled off in different directions. Ranger stayed with the rest of the pack and led us back the way we had come. Sterling had Suki and me follow the path Niall had taken, but at a safe distance.

Niall's nose led him straight to a deer, an old buck. He was grazing silently, then his shoulder twitched. He raised his head and stared at us. Niall looked back at him, asking the same vital question he had asked that moose. With a shiver down my spine, I recognized it.

Is this a good day to die?

My whole body was poised in anticipation. I was aware of the grass tickling my belly, of the deerflies buzzing near my head. I was aware of every leaf, every branch in front of me as I waited for his answer.

The proud deer raised his head even higher and pawed the ground in front of him, as if to show us that he was strong and his life worth asking for. His liquid brown eyes were intelligent and considering, and they said, very clearly, *Yes, you may try.*

He turned then, and I could tell by the way he moved how old he was, how stiff in his limbs, but he bounded away with as much confidence and pride as he must have possessed when young. Niall, Killian, and the others broke into a run. The chase had begun.

A sense of knowledge came from somewhere deep inside my bones. It wasn't the killing that was exciting. It was the game. The thrill of entering into a dangerous contest, one that would most likely end in death. It was a way not just to get food, but to prove our worthiness. And sometimes, like with that giant bull moose, we just didn't measure up. But this buck had found us worthy and was willing to challenge death.

Since we didn't have a task to perform in the hunt, Sterling and Suki and I raced abreast with the buck, but well off to the side. It didn't take long before I realized Niall was skillfully driving him to where he'd ordered the rest of the pack to wait.

I'm sure they heard it before they saw it: a loud crashing through the undergrowth as something ran at a frantic speed. We crashed along next to the buck until he broke through to the pack's hiding place. As soon as he entered the clearing, the rest of the wolves leaped forward. The deer reared up, startled. While he flailed his front hooves at the closest wolf, another leaped toward him from the side and snapped at his rear legs.

The buck stumbled, his front hooves landing on the ground. Another wolf emerged, snapping at his legs from the other side.

The buck whipped his head around, swinging his giant antlers toward the wolves. The wolves backed off a few feet, but didn't leave. They continued to circle their quarry, leaping at the buck with bared teeth, snapping and swiping, weakening him. Suddenly there was a pause, and the buck met Niall's eyes. An acknowledgment passed between them as clearly as if it had been telegraphed throughout the whole forest. The buck found us worthy adversaries and acknowledged our victory.

After that, it was all over in no time at all. As the buck's eyes glazed over with death, they were full of dignity and pride.

20

Niall didn't make those lower in the pack wait too long before they could join in the eating of the kill. I was hugely grateful because another thing I've discovered is that I'm always hungry when I'm in wolf form. Always.

For the next couple of hours, we all gorged ourselves silly. It's amazing to me how my brain can be screaming *no no no,* but my wolf body screams *yes yes yes.* It almost seems to have a mind of its own, as if a part of my normal brain disappears when I'm a wolf. So even while the human part of my brain was saying, *Oh gross, oh gross, do NOT eat that, do you hear me?,* the wolf part of my brain, the much stronger part, at least today, said, *Are you nuts? This is what I live for. This is most excellent,* and then dug right into the deer and, well, feasted. That's the only word for it.

I'll spare you the joys of eating a fresh kill. Unless you are a wolf, you probably won't understand anyway. I will say, though, it is more than just eating. There is a sense of being part of the earth, of the spirit of the deer itself as it shares its life with us. Something I never got from eating a hamburger.

Hours later, when every last strip of meat had been picked clean, and there had been a few arguments over who got to gnaw the bones for the marrow, we all lurched to our feet and began to head for home. My stomach was so full, it was difficult to walk. I wove and stumbled, almost like I was drunk or something. How embarrassing.

I looked up and saw Suki catch herself just before she bumped into a tree. Sterling looked a little shaky himself. Everyone was having the same problem. We were all meat drunk.

The bad news was, it didn't wear off quickly. We all stumbled and fumbled our way toward the village, trusting that Niall knew where he was leading us. The good news was, my body practically hummed with satisfaction from the hunt and the feeding. I've never been so blissfully full in my entire life.

From the angle of the sun, I guessed it was sometime in the early afternoon. I began to recognize where we were. It was some of the same area we'd covered the night of my first transformation. Finally, Niall called a halt and wove his way over to a small clearing. He lowered himself to the ground with a deep sigh of contentment, wrapped himself up with his tail covering his nose, and went to sleep.

With a dizzying sense of relief, the rest of us did the same.

The next thing I knew, someone was shaking me by the shoulder. "Wake up, Luc. Wake up."

For a brief moment, I wondered who Luc was. A few feet away, I heard someone calling for Suki to wake up. Slowly, and with great difficulty, my conscious mind came drifting back to me in clumps and fragments. Oh, yeah. I was Luc. I thought about opening my eyes, but the sun was so bright and the air was so cool, and I wanted to sleep for another day or two.

"Luc!" This time there was a sharpness to the voice, a command that forced my eyes open.

"Huh? What? I'm awake," I said, trying to make it sound convincing.

Niall, who knelt beside me, laughed. "Hardly. But you must wake up. You're supposed to meet Sasha at the cairn and she will have my pelt if you're late."

"Huh?" I said, sitting up. "But that's tomorrow morning."

"It *is* tomorrow morning. Now come. Get up and hurry."

I yawned, and struggled to my feet.

The sun had fully risen by the time I managed to reach the cairn. It was a little eerie, all that stillness combined with the sense of the forest lying there, waiting, breathing, watching. It didn't help that the place was so full of spirits and myths and mystery. I shivered, just a little, and pushed my way through the last break of trees into the clearing.

There it was again. That faint rustling, the sensation of thousands of hands trailing across my skin. Because I knew to expect it, it wasn't nearly as startling as it had been the first time. It also seemed as if the touch lingered more, the voices murmuring more slowly, until I could almost make out individual words.

"Another greeting?" Sasha asked from where she perched on a rock near the cairn.

"Yeah." I let my breath out in a *whoosh*. "I guess I'll get used to that. Eventually."

Sasha uncurled herself off the rock. "I'm sure you're anxious to begin to learn some control over this gift you've been given."

"You can say that again. I'm tired of asking people for help. It's humiliating."

She cocked her head to the side. "Asking for help is humiliating?" She was clearly puzzled.

"Well, yeah. Everyone wants to be independent."

"But then why would you need a pack?" she asked.

"Never mind. So," I said, changing the subject, "you use this place for other stuff besides official ceremonies?"

"Of course. Any of the pack members can come here at any time. Many do. Some come to meditate, others to feel closer to their family members who have passed on. You, too, Luc, should feel free to come here anytime you'd like."

"Okay."

"Now, come stand here, next to me. A little closer to the cairn. That's it." She moved over and made room for me between her and the rocky structure. "Shifting is a combination of meditation, visualization, and controlling your inner self."

I hadn't done real well in the last two weeks managing to control my outer self. Hopefully, the inner part would be easier.

Sasha settled her feet firmly on the forest floor, almost as if she were planting them. "Ground yourself to the earth." Sasha's voice floated through the clearing as soft as a breeze rustling the leaves. I copied what she'd done, setting my feet firmly into the dirt.

"Now, close your eyes and feel the energy flowing up from the very soul of the earth. It will be faint, but if you concentrate, you will feel it. Let it move through the soles of your feet and up your legs, strengthening and elongating the muscles and sinews as it spreads out."

She was right. I could feel the very faintest thread of power, like a superthin, hairy worm crawling through my bones. Which was really nasty if you thought about it. It was hard not to squirm and try to break the connection. The farther up my body the power traveled, the stronger it became. With a slight punch, it hit my gut and it felt like I'd just gone over a really big bump in the road.

Sasha's voice continued: "When it reaches your stomach, use your mind to direct it down your arms, up toward your head. Let it fill every last inch of you, until your whole self is pulsing with the strength of it."

I used my mind to do what she said. I felt the power swallowing up every last bit of me, squeezing through every available space. It almost felt like drowning from the inside out. Just when I was convinced I would burst like a popped balloon, Sasha called out, "Grab your cairn chip, Luc. Touch it and see your wolf self in your mind."

Fumbling, my numb fingers found the little chip of rock. As soon as they made contact, the power began to skitter along the surface of my body, oozing out of my skin and leaving thick gray fur in its wake. With a final excruciating stretch, I felt my arms lengthen until my hands, paws now, rested on the ground. With a shudder that began at my shoulders and spasmed all the way down to my haunches and my tail, I completed the change. I was a wolf.

As always, the world shifted into brighter focus. Everything became more real. I didn't just see the trees, or smell them, but felt them somehow, against my fur.

Sasha laughed. Puzzled, I turned my head toward her. "Oh, Luc. The look of utter surprise on your face was too funny. Don't you realize the more you doubt, the harder you make it? There is no faith needed, no believing. It simply is. Accept it. Enjoy it. But do not doubt it."

21

When I got back to Ranger's house, I went into the kitchen. I wasn't hungry. Wasn't sure I ever would be again. Not after gorging myself on that deer. But instead of finding Ranger fixing breakfast, I found a note.

> Luc,
>
> *Ulric and I are off to the perimeter today. You are to stay with Nuri and keep out of trouble. I'll see you tonight after your lesson in navigation.*
>
> *Ranger*

Perfect. That was exactly what I'd planned to do anyway.

It didn't take long to reach Nuri's. Just before I knocked, he stuck his head out the window right above me. "I'll be down in just a couple of minutes."

"Okay." As I stepped back from the door, it opened. "Boy, I knew you could move fast, but—"

My mouth snapped shut. It wasn't Nuri. Not exactly. It

was a miniature version of him, maybe eight years old or so. He had the same red hair, freckles, and cinnamon-colored eyes, but was seriously lacking in the height department. "Hi," I said.

The kid gave me the once-over, and I felt myself grow embarrassed. What was he looking at, anyway? I was just about to growl at him to back off when Nuri came through the door, shoving the kid out of the way. "Leave him alone, Devo. He's not a freak."

Devo shrugged. "If you say so." He looked like he had his doubts.

Nuri said, "Come on," and began walking toward the village.

"You're going to get in trouble again, aren't you?" Devo called after him. "If you take me with you, I won't tell."

"Good try, Devo," Nuri called back, "but not a chance." The kid shrugged and went back inside.

"So," I said as I caught up with Nuri. "*Are* we going to get in trouble today?"

"Nah. He just wanted me to think he had something on me. That's all. Plus, I usually end up in trouble, so it was an easy guess."

"Oh," I said, disappointed. I was kind of in the mood for trouble. Everyone was in a bad mood around here anyway; might as well get some fun out of it. "So where're we going, then?"

"To the perimeter," Nuri said, grinning.

I smiled. "Excellent."

Nuri gave a giant *whoop* and began to run toward the trees. Being the good friend that I was, I followed. Didn't want him getting in trouble all by himself.

We'd only gone a little ways when Nuri stopped and turned around so suddenly that I nearly bumped into him. "What?" I said, wondering if someone had spotted us already.

"You know, this will be a lot more fun if we're in our wolf shapes. Can you change yet?"

I thought about the lesson Sasha had given me. "Yeah. I think so. And if not, you can lend me some of your power, right?"

Nuri looked sheepish. "Well, alone, I'm not so good at that. Don't have enough focus. Suki is the one that knows how to channel all that stuff."

"Well, I'll try it alone, then."

"Right. I'll wait and see if you can do it before I change." Nuri took a few steps back and settled in to watch.

I began the visualization exercises that Sasha had taught me. I forced myself to focus and envisioned my wolf shape, the fur sprouting from my body, my bones and muscles elongating. I could sense my wolf spirit, deep inside, swimming back and forth like an enormous goldfish trapped in too small a bowl. "You know," I finally said, "I can't do this with you watching me."

"Oh. Sorry." Nuri turned to face the trees.

I closed my eyes again, called up the visuals, and clutched the cairn chip—hard. I felt the energy prickle its way down my arm toward my gut. It spread out, through my limbs, then with a giant flutter and a lurch, the goldfish burst out of the bowl, and I changed shape.

"Excellent," Nuri said, turning around. In about two seconds flat, he was in his wolf shape. The show-off.

The perimeter was much farther from the village than I would have guessed. Farther, even, than Nuri had been that first time I'd seen him running alongside Ranger's car. As I loped along in my wolf form, I felt the tension and confusion of the last three days disappear. It suddenly didn't matter what secrets Ranger or my grandfather was keeping. It didn't matter what Rolfe thought, and I couldn't care less about Latin, or Teague, or this whole Alpha authority thing.

We ran and ran, stretching our legs and bodies their full length. We took our time, pausing to smell something interesting or chase a rabbit who got in our way.

Nuri took me to the edge of our pack's territory and showed me one of the sentinel stones. It was a pile of rocks, a lot like the ones at the cairn, stacked about four feet high. I leaned forward and sniffed. Immediately a picture of Ulric with the pack standing around him came into my mind. The sense of them was so strong, the stones nearly hummed with it. When I tried to cross the boundary line, I felt a buzzing along my body, a nerve-racking vibration. I quickly retreated back inside the boundaries.

Nuri grew bored with the sentinel stones pretty quickly. Me, I could have stood there for hours and tried to puzzle them out. In the end, Nuri won, mostly because he was going to leave without me. With a snap at my hind legs, he turned and ran.

I gave chase, like I was supposed to, enjoying the feel of the wind through my fur. Up ahead I saw Nuri check his speed, turn in my direction, and launch himself straight at me.

I didn't even have enough warning to slow down. He plowed into my side, knocking me off my feet, so that we both tumbled round and round. When we came to a stop, I sat up, shook the leaves out of my ears, and looked at him.

He grinned back and wagged his tail.

Slowly, my mouth widened into a smile. It *had* been fun. Exactly like a Ferris wheel. Only better.

Nuri dropped low, creeping along the ground in my direction with a gleam in his eye.

I got into the spirit of the thing and crouched, ready to spring.

He launched at me with a growl, and soon we were a tangle of limbs and jaws snapping and yipping, having the time of our lives.

We separated, slowly circling each other, low snarls pulling our lips back from our teeth. Something, a noise, flicked against my ear and I paused, trying to hear what it was.

Big mistake. Another *thud* and eighty pounds of Nuri caught me in the chest, sending me on a backward roll that stopped when I slammed into a tree trunk. *Yeouwf!* I barked. Enough. I shook my head clear, then lifted it, my whole body tense and still. Then I heard it again.

Carried on the wind came a lone distant howl so full of anguish and pain that it raised the hairs on the back of my neck.

Nuri and I froze, then, before conscious thought set in, we launched ourselves toward the distress call.

I threw myself forward and streaked past trees, darting under the branches and veering around fallen logs. The power in my body shocked me, went way beyond anything I could ever have imagined.

I smelled him before I saw him. The rich coppery tang of blood danced on the air. He was Lycanthian. And he was wounded. An accident? No, an attack, I corrected as my brain processed the smell of fear, adrenaline, and shock.

I checked my speed. We needed to approach with more caution. Nuri looked over at me and I motioned for him to hang back. The smell of blood and pain grew thicker now. And worry. We slunk to our bellies and crawled forward. My ears picked up the sound of labored breathing. I tensed, trying to listen for any sound of pursuit or further threat, but I heard nothing.

At last we came upon the injured wolf, an enormous black male sitting on his haunches, struggling to keep upright. Three bright, red gashes ran down his side. Blood pooled on the ground beside him.

I whined high up in my throat, alerting him to our arrival and intentions. He gave a quick sharp whine back, then fell silent. With a start, I realized he smelled familiar. I didn't think I'd ever set eyes on him before, but somehow my nose knew him.

Since Nuri knew the woods better than I, we decided he would run back to get help while I stayed with the wounded wolf.

Pausing barely long enough to catch his breath, Nuri turned and dashed back off through the trees.

I settled myself on the ground next to the stranger. I sniffed his wounds, trying to see how bad they were. They were deep and had a particular smell to them that made my nose hurt.

His breathing was labored, quick shallow pants. He whined high in his throat, then gave a growling yap. I could tell he was trying to warn against something, but I was too stupid to know what.

I whined back, trying to reassure him. I drew closer so he could sniff me, hoping that would make him feel better. As we waited, it felt like the forest drew itself around us, pulling us close, doing its best to keep us safe. I tried to make myself as small as possible.

A short while later, a howl came through the trees. Nuri. He'd found Ranger and Ulric and they were on their way. Some of the tension left me.

I heard them coming now, the light rapid sound of their paws hitting the forest floor. Seconds later, they broke into the small clearing where I sat next to the wounded wolf.

With a quick shimmer and swirl, Ranger shifted from his wolf shape to his human one and immediately knelt beside the stranger. I backed up to give him room as the other wolves and men drew closer.

"Kevin!" Ranger barked out. "Help Loki with the stretcher. Sloan! You go find Kora. Tell her to be ready to get to work as soon as we get Remus back to the village." Ranger's voice was filled with such cold fury that I shivered.

"Any idea who attacked him?" Nuri asked as he hovered nearby.

"This is Fenriki from the Mabon Pack who called on me Tuesday. My guess would be abolitionists."

Remus barked. Ranger leaned closer. "Later, Remus. When we have you safe and comfortable."

Just then, Kevin and Loki reappeared with the stretcher. Four men picked Remus up and gently laid him on the stretcher. When he was finally secure, Ranger grabbed one end and Ulric grabbed the other. They headed back to the village at a steady clip. The rest of us followed.

Kora, the old healing woman, was waiting for us in her doorway. "Bring him right in. I've got a bed ready." She motioned the stretcher inside, and the rest of us crowded in the doorway behind them. Still in wolf shape, I nosed my way in.

Kora motioned everyone back, but didn't make us leave. Ulric and Ranger set Remus on the bed, then Ranger knelt beside him. The rest of us stood back against the wall. The smell of blood hung heavy in the air, coppery, slightly sweet, and thick with warmth. An undercoating of fear lay beneath it.

Kora looked at Ulric. "Can you help him change?"

"I can try," Ulric said. "Although, since he's from a different pack, it won't be easy."

Someone moved through the crowd, and Sasha appeared next to the bed. "Perhaps if we both tried." She and Ulric exchanged a glance, and in that moment, I had a glimpse of true unity, of a complete, equal sharing of concerns and responsibility.

Ulric placed his hands on the stranger's temples, and Sasha placed her hands on top of Ulric's. Sasha spoke softly. "Remus, we're going to help you change so that our healer can take care of you. You have been given safety by the Golwyg Pack. Relax and help us if you can, but if not, do not fight it. You are safe here." She nodded at Ulric, and they both closed their eyes.

The air began to shimmer around the two of them, like static electricity. It was colorless, but there was a quivering in the air that reached out and encircled the injured shifter. The wolf's fur began to stand on end, almost as if it were being held up to a vacuum cleaner. Taller and taller it stretched until it began to pull at the skin as well. The sensation was so strong I felt it in my own body. There was a *whoosh* and a swirl, then it was as if his wolf shape was sucked from his body, like a husk, leaving a large, unconscious human body behind. Dizzy myself, I blinked, surprised to find that I had also changed back into human form.

I looked back over at the bed, then gasped. I knew that body! It was Ogre Bill. From the café Ranger and I stopped at on the night we left the city.

Kora slipped forward and studied the three slashes on Remus's ribs. They were deep and ugly. Ranger watched over her shoulder.

"Made with silver blades," Kora told Ranger without looking up.

He nodded. "I was afraid of that. Otherwise, they would have begun to heal by now."

A voice exploded from the crowd. "I told you you were risking our safety again!" It was Sloan, Rolfe's father, and he looked darkly at me. With a growl that shook my eardrums, Ulric turned, strode toward him, and shoved the other man outside.

"They're close. Too close." Remus's weak voice rose up from the bed. "They came into the café, then tried to follow me."

"How many are there?" Ranger asked.

"There were two. Now there are none." Remus's words hung in the air as we all absorbed the weight of them.

"You've done well," Ulric said, patting the injured man's leg. "Very well."

"Enough talking," Kora ordered. She lifted an ornate crystal decanter from the bedside table and poured some of the contents onto a soft piece of white cloth. The liquid was as clear as water, and it smelled faintly of moonlight. Kora turned to tend to her patient.

As she worked at the wound on his side, she seemed to remember she had a room full of people watching. She paused. "Go on out, all of you. I'll do all I can for him, then rest will serve him best. That and the nearness of the pack. Sasha will sit with him first, then the rest of you can take turns until he is healed. Now go on. Out."

She made shooing motions with her hands, and we all trooped from the room. Since I had been one of the first in, I had to wait while everyone else filed out in front of me. When I finally got outside, I found Sterling, Ranger, and Ulric huddled together talking in quiet voices. "You must look into this," Ulric told Ranger.

Ranger nodded. "I know where Remus was patrolling. I'll speak to the Mabon Pack, then go see what I can find."

"What about me?" I blurted out, forgetting myself. I flinched inwardly, expecting Ulric to scold me for intruding, but he didn't.

"You will stay with your grandfather," Ulric said.

Ranger nodded his agreement. "Very well." He came over to me. "Until I return, then," he said, and ruffled my hair.

Then he left.

22

Things were very quiet the next two days. It was as if the whole pack were holding its breath, waiting. Waiting to see if the wounded Fenriki would be all right. Waiting to see if Ranger would return safely. Waiting to see if there would be other attacks. We all focused our thoughts on healing and safe return. When we went back to school on Monday, Teague took it easy on us and stuck with literature, mostly telling us all the old tales he loved so well. But hey, at least it wasn't Latin.

When school was finally finished, I went outside and waited for Suki. Sterling had told me to spend the afternoon with her since he was busy working on some charts and maps for Ulric. When Suki caught up to me, she explained we were working with Kora today. One of us would help her collect herbs, and the other would sit with Remus until they got back.

We turned to head toward Kora's cabin, swerving to avoid a small group of juveniles who were standing around talking in low voices. When Rolfe saw me, he smirked and kicked a stone with his foot. Of course it just happened to come skittering over to me.

I immediately went on alert, and I felt Suki grow tense.

"Happy now?" he muttered.

I stared back. This was the first time he'd confronted me since I'd trounced him the night of my changing ceremony. "What are you talking about? Why would I be happy about this?"

Suki's eyes flashed fire. "Be quiet, Rolfe!"

Rolfe took two steps toward us, his fists clenched. "Why are you protecting him, Suki? He's nothing but a lousy traitor."

I froze. "How'd you get traitor?"

He looked up at me and gave me a really nasty smile. The hairs on the back of my neck stood up, and my gut twisted.

"Because you've brought the abolitionists right to our door. Again."

I gaped at him, my mind hardly able to process his words. "What are you talking about?"

"The abolitionists aren't here by accident."

"Quiet, Rolfe," Nuri warned with a low growl.

Rolfe turned and snarled at him. "If he's one of us, he needs to know the truth."

"But not this way," Suki said.

I glanced at Suki. "No! I'm tired of everyone keeping the truth from me." I turned back to Rolfe. "So what do you mean, the abolitionists aren't here by accident?"

"It's your uncle. He's sent them after you. Again."

"Again?" I repeated.

"Yeah. Like before, when he came after you when you were little. The time the abolitionists killed your father."

Rolfe's words hit me like a fist. "Wait, wait, wait," I cried out. "My father died in a car accident." I stared into all their faces. Some looked at me with pity, others with anger, and a few, like Rolfe, with hatred.

"It's true," Suki whispered, wringing her hands.

I shook my head and backed away. "Are you trying to tell me that my uncle Stephen, the guy I lived with for the last nine years, sent abolitionists out here to kill my father?"

"Not just your father. All of us." Rolfe's eyes were hard with hatred, but I finally understood it.

"Your uncle was their informant," Rolfe said. "If it wasn't for him, they never would have gotten so close. And now they're back." He turned his head and spat in disgust. "No true Lycanthian could ever forgive someone for that. They wouldn't have lived with him for nine years. They would have ripped his throat out and feasted on his entrails."

My gut twisted. I couldn't breathe. I couldn't think. This wasn't true. But even as I stood there and denied it, I could feel my whole world crashing down around me. "No," I said. "No!"

I turned and ran, blindly at first. Then I realized that my feet were taking me to Sterling's house.

23

I burst into my grandfather's house, the front door crashing against the wall. My grandfather's head snapped up.

He sat at a small table in the dining area with a huge map and charts spread out before him.

"Tell me." I could barely get the words out. My heart was jackhammering in my chest, and I was breathing hard and fast. I strode across the room. "Is it true?"

Slowly, my grandfather took off his glasses. "Is what true?"

"Well, it depends," I said. "Just how many lies did you guys tell me?"

He gave a low, warning growl. "We told you no lies, Luc."

"Excuse me. I should ask, How many things did you forget to tell me?"

"Watch yourself! I am an elder, and I am superior to you. Now what is all this about?"

"Rolfe said that Stephen sent the abolitionists to kill my father. Is that true?" It was a struggle to get the words out, as if saying them made them more true.

At the mention of Stephen's name, my grandfather's lips drew back slightly. I felt his anger prickle along the back of my neck. He threw his pen down on the table with such force that it skittered along the surface and rolled off the other end. "Yes," he said at last. "It's true."

True. It was true. They'd known all along and hidden it from me. "Why didn't you or Ranger tell me? Don't you think I have a right to know?"

"Luc, you've already had so much thrown at you in the last few days. We thought it best to wait awhile. Besides, it happened long ago."

"Just because it happened in the past doesn't mean it doesn't matter," I almost shouted. I took a deep breath. "Stephen"—I couldn't bring myself to call him uncle anymore—"betrayed my father? To his death?" The words were so hard to say, I almost choked on them.

Sterling's shoulders slumped. "Yes. Remember the band of bounty hunters that I told you had come into our territory to hunt us out? The ones who killed your grandmother?"

I nodded.

"Well, they weren't bounty hunters, but abolitionists." My grandfather stood up and went to look out his window, as if unwilling to look at me. "Your mother had been very sick. Cancer. She and your father had been in the city for medical treatment. They were on their way back when they were ambushed just outside of Lost Pines."

"Why? How?"

"Stephen was furious that Sara wouldn't stay in the city, closer to the doctors. He felt that if Kennet were dead, she'd have no choice but to stay with him and be nearer to the hospital. So he turned to the abolitionists. He lied and told them a werewolf had kidnapped his sister and was heading east toward the pass. He gave them Kennet's license-plate number, and the abolitionists caught up with him by the time he reached Lost Pines.

"Luckily for us, he was able to evade them long enough to change shape and howl out a warning that the Mabon picked up and immediately relayed. We hurried to Lost Pines, but we were too late.

"They'd sent four hit squads into the area. They didn't know the exact location of our village, but knew they were close.

"For three long days, we were both hunter and hunted as we tracked the hit squads and eliminated them. Many Lycanthians died, including your grandmother."

I stumbled to a chair and eased myself into it. With a painful jolt, I realized that's when Stephen had begun to actively hate me. When he saw the signs that I was part Lycanthian. "And you didn't think this was important enough to tell me?"

"Of course it's important! Almost more so than any of us can bear. But the pain and destruction Stephen caused have already cost us too much. At some point, for the good of the pack, we have to put it aside."

"Why?"

"Do you know how many we have already lost to this madness? Your grandmother; your father; Rolfe's mother;

Wade, the previous Fenriki; the list goes on. Eight of our pack were killed."

No wonder Rolfe hated me. Stephen had been responsible for his mother's death.

I jerked my head up to look at him. "And how could you have let me go off with him? Knowing what you did?"

"Because your mother was still alive. The abolitionists didn't harm her. They took her, and you, back to Stephen in trade for the information he'd given them."

"But then—"

"She died three weeks later, of the cancer that plagued her."

My grandfather turned around, his face looking ten years older than when I had first stepped into the room. "We had no choice but to let you stay with Stephen." Sterling shook his head. "He threatened to expose us to the courts, and tell them what we were. They would have denied us custody then. We couldn't risk the safety of the entire pack for one child. Especially since we knew you'd be safe until your thirteenth birthday. And Ranger checked on you periodically."

"He did?"

Sterling turned to the window and looked out across the backyard. "Many times. On his travels into the city, he would stop and look in on you. Stephen never knew, of course, and neither did you, apparently, but it helped us all to know you were safe and growing well."

"But now Stephen has done it again," I said, feeling sick. "That's what all the increased patrols are about, aren't they?"

"We suspect that's the case, yes. Neither Stephen nor the abolitionists know our exact location." Sterling nodded toward the maps he was studying. "But they are getting dangerously close."

"What will happen if the abolitionists find us?" I asked.

"We will fight to the death in order to save ourselves. It won't be the first time in our history that we've had to fight for our very existence."

I fell silent, digesting all that he had told me. The responsibility for having brought all this misery to the Lycanthians weighed heavily on me. I hated knowing that this was my fault. I hated knowing that I had lived side by side with Stephen for nine years when he had betrayed my father to his death. How could I ever face any of the pack again?

A vivid and brilliant anger burst inside my head, like Fourth of July fireworks, nearly blinding me.

Stephen had betrayed my father. The words were branded in my brain like red-hot coals against the soft tissue. I could see nothing but those words, hear nothing but those words. My whole world narrowed down to that one thought. *He can't get away with this.* I turned and stumbled toward the door. *I won't let him.*

"Luc! Wait!" my grandfather called, but I barely heard him.

Anger warred with despair. Despair warred with grief. Fury sat side by side with pain so deep I didn't think it would ever end. I heard Sterling call me again, but kept moving away from his cottage. I didn't want to talk now. I didn't want to talk, or think, or feel. I took a step, then another. By the time my grandfather reached the front porch, I was running down the center of the village.

I ran toward the trees, dark shadows against the deepening dusk. The swirling mass of my emotions soon settled into one.

Rage.

Without my even trying, my humanness fell away until there was nothing left but motion and instinct streaking through the forest.

24

I raced through the trees. The wind rushed through my fur, cooling me a little so that my rage sat like a banked fire. But it was there, smoldering, waiting for the slightest motion to fan it back into a blaze.

Stephen had to pay. Surely the authorities would listen to me. I'd lived in Seattle forever. I'd gone to school there, known people. But who should I call? The police? A lawyer? There had to be some way to bring Stephen to justice.

And then it hit me. I was thinking like a human. But I was a Lycanthian. I could do this. *I* could bring Stephen to justice. I had the strength and the power to deal with him. I could cover a hundred miles a day, hitting top speeds of forty miles per hour. I had jaws that could crack a two-by-four like it was a corn nut, forty-two teeth, designed to pierce through bone. I didn't need the law. I didn't even need the other shape-shifters. It was *my* father Stephen had betrayed. It was because of *me* the whole village was in danger. *I* should be the one to deal with it.

And I would.

Houses and buildings began to cluster together. A town. I was approaching another town. I'd passed two during the night, but they'd been small and easy to avoid. This one was bigger.

I slowed my pace and clung to the darkness of the night, instinct warning me to stay hidden. It was near daybreak. I could feel it in the way the breeze shifted, the slight rise in temperature as it ruffled the ends of my fur, and the faint lessening of the darkness.

I hadn't thought about how to get through the populated areas. I hadn't thought about much of anything except finding Stephen. And avenging my father's death.

A light flicked on in a nearby house. I cringed back against the welcoming darkness of the trees. A nearby dog picked up my scent and began barking. The *woof woof woof* raised my hackles. I wanted to find that dog and make it stop. I wanted to stare into its eyes and see it cower in submission.

I'd taken two steps forward before I realized what I was doing and forced myself back into the shadow. The wolf instincts were becoming stronger the longer I stayed in my wolf form. I would have to watch myself.

I switched directions and headed north of the town to see if I could avoid it altogether. My nose picked up the clean, sharp scent of water. A large body of water. A lake. It would take too long to go around. I turned back and went south. Maybe I could get around that way, but the sound of cars and the smell of asphalt told me there was a highway in that direction. Too dangerous.

Turning back, I cut through the edge of the town closest to the lake. This early in the morning, with the weather growing colder by the day, there wouldn't be many people out. Or so I hoped. I was uneasy at the different smells. It was almost like a physical warning telling me to get out. But I couldn't. I kept going forward, determined to ignore the unfamiliar scents, hoping that my senses would alert me to any problem before I stepped into the middle of it.

I slunk between the trees and the shadows until I cleared the small town. There was a wide expanse of woods between the lake and the highway, so I kept to that, staying hidden as best I could.

When the sun finally crested the eastern peaks, I realized I would have to find cover for the day. I had run through the night, and was only now beginning to tire. But a wolf would be too easy to spot in the broad daylight. I didn't want to be shot, or whatever else people did when they spotted wolves running wild among them.

I stopped, lifted my nose to the wind, and caught a whiff of rock and cold, damp air. A cave. Not too far, either. I followed the scent until I found a small hollow in the ground. Using my nose, I checked for current inhabitants. I caught the scent of man, but it was faint, from long ago. Months. Perhaps even years. My nostrils flared as I caught the sharp scent of cougar. I sniffed more closely and found that it, too, had faded. The most recent scent was that of raccoons, a small family of them. They weren't here now, and if they returned while I slept, well, I wasn't worried. They would wait until I was gone before venturing back into their home.

I found the softest-looking spot on the cave floor, circled it three times, then flopped down with a deep sigh. I settled my head on my aching paws and faced the opening of the cave. My breathing slowed, I closed my eyes, and I drifted off to the inviting abyss of sleep.

As the sun began to set, I got under way. It was smooth sailing until I reached Stuberville, a small city about ninety miles northeast of Seattle.

I was surprised at how much my wolf body hated the city, even a small one. The sounds were loud and violent against my ears, the smells so foul they nearly choked me. Even though I was the original city boy, I found myself longing for the cool pine forests, the deep quiet of a night in the wilderness, burbling brooks, and lots of furry bodies around me.

I slunk through the city streets, trying to keep to the shadows and take the shortest possible route through the concrete-and-brick obstacle course. There were so many people! It was hard to keep out of sight, and there was just no way to explain the presence of a wild wolf strolling through city streets. I thought about returning to my human shape, but realized I had no idea how to do it by myself. I'd always had help before. I fought off a flutter of panic.

A large group of people, loud and reeking of beer, stumbled by my hiding place, their voices raised in laughing conversation. I cringed back and waited for them to pass before darting to the next shadow. At this rate, it was going to take me two days to get out of Stuberville and back onto the open road.

There was a sound behind me, like a foot making contact with a rock or tin can. I turned, but couldn't see anyone. I sniffed the air, but I was upwind, so I couldn't detect the source of the noise. It was probably just one of the loud party-goers stumbling as they walked. There were so many noises in the city: loud ones, faint ones, some close and others nearly two miles away. It was hard to focus on one sound at a time.

I moved forward again and studied my choices. I was on a partially lit street, and light was my enemy. To my left, a dark alleyway gaped onto the street like a giant black mouth. Perfect. All that darkness looked like good cover.

I crept out from my hiding place and slunk toward the shadow cast by a parked car. I checked for traffic and any-one who might see me. The street loomed to either side of me, empty, silent. A few streetlights threw off pools of weak light. I lifted my muzzle and sniffed the night air again, trying to see if there was anything out there. All I could smell was asphalt, gasoline, rotting food, and bad sewer drainage.

I gathered my muscles, then sprang from behind the car. Dashing from shadow to shadow, I avoided the pools of light as I made my way to the alley.

As I stepped into the darkness, I heaved a sigh of relief. No shouts had gone up, no alarms sounded about some wolf running wild in the streets of Stuberville. But I needed to get moving. I set off at a trot, hoping my instinct for direction would be good enough.

Fifty yards into the alley, I heard a sound that made me freeze. It was the sole of a shoe. And it crunched ever so quietly on a piece of gravel or glass. It was unnaturally quiet. Like someone was trying to avoid being heard.

My hackles raised. A growl rose in my throat. It took all my willpower to tamp it back down. Silence was what I needed now.

I slunk back against the wall. There was another footstep. As soft as falling snow, but I'd heard it. Someone was behind me. And they were working very hard at being quiet.

My nose picked up the scent of humans, leather, and sweat. From the scent of the sweat, I caught four distinctly different odors. There were at least four different people. Men, actually. Whoever was coming toward me was nervous and amped up. Didn't seem like a good combination. But, boy, wouldn't they be surprised when they tried to mug someone and it turned out to be a wolf with claws and sharp teeth.

That thought calmed me down a little bit. Humans, even four of them, couldn't really harm me. I was faster, a better predator. My instincts were more finely honed. Still, it didn't seem smart to stick around and wait for them to show up. It seemed like a good time to put on a burst of wolf speed.

I leaped from the shadows and began running down the alley, all speed and graceful motion, loving the feel of my muscles as they worked effortlessly, my adrenaline pumping at the threat of confrontation.

Surprised shouts and voices erupted behind me. I ignored them as I raced along toward the end of the alley. I should be able to escape without these guys even getting a close look at me.

I quickened my pace, then skidded to a stop when I saw the brick wall looming before me.

The alley was a dead end.

25

Once I stopped running, I could hear the men behind me better. They were running also, loudly and clumsily. I hadn't wanted to fight them, or show myself, but now I didn't have any choice.

I crouched in the dark, ready to spring. My lips were pulled back to show off my fangs to their best advantage.

When the first fellow got close enough for me to see, I froze. He was dressed all in black leather, from head to toe. He had huge, spiked leather bands around his neck and wrists. I caught a tingling metallic scent on the air and realized the spikes weren't just metal. They were silver.

I had my first moment of true fear.

They were all dressed the same. Black leather and silver spikes that went way beyond hard-core Goth.

I snarled, showing my teeth and raising my hackles.

"Come on, wolfie. You get good and mad."

Wolfie?

The others fanned out behind the leader, coming toward me on either side. One slunk along the far wall until he was behind me. I was surrounded. I remembered the Lycanthian code. No harm to humans except in case of extreme self-defense. Well, four armed men against one inexperienced wolf seemed like extreme self-defense to me.

Metal scraped against leather, and the scent of silver grew stronger. I glanced over my shoulder. The man back there had drawn a huge silver knife from a sheath at his hip.

A sinister whisper cut through the night as the others drew their knives.

I had to stay away from those vicious silver blades. I kept my eyes focused on the guy in front of me, like I was getting ready to attack him, then launched myself to the right, trying to dodge between two of the men.

"Get him!" the leader shouted. They rushed me. The night became a blurred confusion of motion and silver and swinging limbs. I swiped at the chest of the man in front of me, my claws shredding the black leather like tissue paper and sinking into the flesh beneath. The man screamed and stepped back, four lines of red appearing on his chest.

An arm grabbed me by the neck. I started to bite the hand, wanting to maim it beyond recognition, but the silver stopped me, repelled me like a magnet or Kryptonite or something. As much as I wanted to bite down on that wrist, I couldn't. When I hesitated, bodies moved toward me, grabbing my legs. I thrashed against their hold, my whole body twisting and turning, trying to force them to let go. But whenever I tried to use my teeth, the silver spikes were there, stopping me cold.

"Hurry up!"

One of the men stepped closer, pointing his knife directly at my throat. "Keep him still! I don't want to get bit!"

"This is as still as he's going to get! Now do it!"

Panic seized me, and I started struggling again, trying to escape their hold. I got my teeth around someone's forearm where there were no vicious silver spikes, and bit down. Hard. Someone screamed, and the arm loosened. Then someone threw a leg over me to pin me down.

"Hold still, wolf," a low voice commanded. "You should be thanking us. Once we remove your pelt, you'll no longer be an abomination."

Pelt? He wanted to remove my pelt?

I watched, mesmerized as the sharp point of the knife drew closer. I felt the powerful hum of the silver pulsing against me.

The silver tip bit into my flesh with a burning, ripping sensation that made me scream. The feel of the silver was like a horrible electric shock buzzing down my shoulder. Panicking, I felt my eyes grow wide and roll up in my sockets as I thrashed against the arms that held me.

Just as someone yelled, "Hold him!" I felt a cool rush of power trickle across my skin.

Ranger.

I saw Ranger's arm snake across the throat of my assailant. At the same time, he reached out and twisted the knife from the man's hand so hard and fast I heard the bones shatter.

The man screamed. "You broke my hand!"

Ranger could move almost faster than the eye could see. Before the others had a chance to realize what was happening, he kicked the leg of the man holding me. I heard a sickening snap as the man's knee broke, then suddenly I was free as he collapsed to the ground.

That was all I needed. I ripped myself out of the second man's hold and leaped to my feet. The other two faced Ranger, their silver knives winking wickedly in the faint light. Ranger stood, knees slightly bent, holding the silver knife he'd taken from the first attacker.

The two men advanced on Ranger. I leaped forward, clamping my jaws down on the forearm of the man closest to me. His knife dropped uselessly to the ground. Digging my teeth in deeper, I shook his arm, almost as if I was trying to tear it off. The silver spikes were right there, jerking back and forth, and so close to my jaw I could practically taste them.

Using his free arm, my assailant reached out and whacked me upside the head with his wrist. Pain, vivid and brilliant, burst inside my head like poisoned darts. I dropped his arm. Where the silver had made contact with me, it felt as if someone had shoved an electrically charged metallic rod into my skull.

I shook my head, trying to dislodge some of the pain and remember how to think. When my eyes cleared, I found Ranger holding the knife to the throat of the man whose knee he'd shattered. Footsteps pounded in the distance as the others ran away.

"Who sent you?" Ranger asked.

"No one. It was just a regular patrol."

"Liar!" Ranger grabbed the man by the hair and shook him. "I can smell the lies on you. Who sent you? And consider your answer carefully, because my hand is getting tired of holding this knife. It would be a shame if it slipped."

There was a long, tense moment of silence while the man considered his answer. "We got an anonymous tip to expect increased werewolf activity in this area."

Ranger growled, then shook the man again. "What other *tips* have you heard?"

"O-only to be on the lookout for increased were-wolf activity. Th-that something big would be coming down soon. A raid maybe? We were told to be ready for it, that's all."

Ranger studied the man to see if he was telling the truth. When he was finally convinced, Ranger gave a little nod, then cocked his elbow back and struck the man in the temple. He crumpled to the ground, unconscious.

I stared at Ranger.

"We need to get away. I don't want him following us and identifying my car. He'll be fine in a few hours, except for the knee and a bad headache. Now come on. We need to get out of here."

As I slunk along after him, I was suddenly very embarrassed. Having to face Ranger with what I'd done and the trouble I'd caused him seemed much more terrifying than a whole alleyful of attackers.

When we reached the street, I saw his SUV was pulled up halfway on the curb. He'd parked in a hurry. He turned and saw me looking, and his eyes scorched me with his anger and frustration. "Hopefully, a silver spike to the side of your head, and the pain it brings you, will serve as a reminder of just how incredibly stupid and dangerous this was." He opened the passenger door for me. "Now get in."

As I hopped up onto the seat, he got in on the other side.

I jumped when his fist hit the steering wheel. "Do you know who those men were back there?"

I shook my head and whined low in my throat.

"An abolitionist hit squad. That's who.

"If I hadn't come along when I did . . . And I cannot believe you came into town when you can't even control your own shifting!"

I just hung my head.

He took a deep breath to calm himself. "I'm going to help you shift back. Ready?"

I nodded, and he reached out and placed his hand across my eyes, touching at each of my temples, like he had the last time. "Picture yourself in human form, Luc. Envision your legs, your arms, your whole body, then finally your head," he said softly.

I could feel my humanness being pulled up from some murky place deep in my soul.

While I sat for a moment, trying to catch my breath and orient myself, I asked the first question that popped into my mind. "How did you find me?"

"As soon as I arrived back at the village, before I'd even come to a complete stop, Sterling, Luna, Nuri, and Ulric were gathering around the car, talking all at once. When I got everyone to calm down, they told me what had happened. That you had found out the truth of your father's death and had gone looking for vengeance."

And try as hard as I might, I couldn't ignore the feeling of warmth at the knowledge that the pack had been so concerned for me. "But how did you physically find me?"

He turned and looked at me, his amber eyes eerie in the dim light from the streetlamps. "I tracked you. I followed your scent trail, and when I got close enough, I listened for you. Just because I'm in my human shape doesn't mean I don't have access to my wolf abilities."

"Do you think it was Uncle Stephen who tipped the abolitionists off? Like last time?"

He turned and stared out of the windshield. "I think he may have been the anonymous tip, yes."

He turned back to me, his eyes cold. "Are you still set on this course of action?"

I remembered Sterling's aching sorrow, the empty place inside me where my father should have been, my new-found strength and power. From deep inside, the jagged edges of my rage lifted and stirred. "Yes. I am going, with you or without you."

Ranger sighed heavily. "Very well."

"Why the sad face? You can't care about Stephen after all he's done?"

He was so quiet at first that I thought he wasn't going to answer. "No," he finally said. "But I've seen how high a price revenge has cost our pack, and I am loath to pay more than we already have."

26

Ranger parked his SUV a few blocks away from the condo where I used to live. It seemed like six lifetimes ago, not eight days.

Saying nothing, we walked through the heavy mist. When we reached Stephen's condo, Ranger pulled me back into the shadows. "What is your plan?"

I turned to him. "Plan? The plan is to go in there and make him pay for betraying my father. The plan is to pay him back for all the pack members whose deaths he's responsible for. That's the plan."

Ranger sighed again. "That is no plan, that is an impulse."

When I glared at him, he continued. "Do you plan to confront him in wolf form or human? Will you go through the window or knock on the front door? What will you do if he has company? What if Jane is there? Will she be the object of your revenge as well?"

"Did she betray my father?"

Ranger shook his head. "No. She was much grieved. I

think the only reason she didn't leave Stephen was because of you. She wanted to stay and help you."

My eyes wanted to go all warm and soft, but I kept them cold and hard. "Fine. Then she's out of it. The rest I'll worry about later."

Ranger was quiet for a moment. "Do you intend to kill him?"

I stared at Ranger, his words making it real for the first time. *Did* I intend to kill Stephen? He deserved death, since that's what he'd given my father.

"If you kill him in front of Jane," Ranger said quietly, "will she call the police? Will she send the police after you? After the pack? Right now most people either don't know about us or don't believe we exist. How will the pack fare if you bring a mob of police, all screaming for our blood, down about their ears? Will you not have just traded one massacre for another?"

My resolve faltered slightly then. I did not want harm to come to the pack. They were my family. But Stephen couldn't go unpunished. At least not while I had the power to right wrongs. "If I don't do something, Stephen will end up bringing even more harm to the pack. Won't he?"

Ranger's steely eyes bored into mine. "We have a good chance of keeping Stephen and his abolitionist friends from finding our village or hurting our people. They only know that we are somewhere beyond Lost Pines, and that wilderness is vast. Our patrols can prevent them from ever locating our village. But a full-scale manhunt with the power of the law behind it . . ." He shook his head. "The police have weapons and manpower and resources the abolitionists don't. Our risk of harm would be much greater. Think about that as you plan your revenge."

Then he turned and led me through the shadows to the back of the condo.

The downstairs was ablaze with lights, the second floor dark. We crept toward the living-room window, which was covered with wooden blinds. Luckily for us, they weren't closed all the way. We could see into the room in little inch-wide slots.

Uncle Stephen was there, and he was alone. It took me a moment to realize he was talking on his cell phone.

He sounded furious. "You found one in Stuberville? What do you mean he got away? That could have been Luc! How long ago was that?"

There was a long pause, then he spoke again. "Well, find him! And let me know as soon as you do."

So Stephen *had* tipped the abolitionists off. It was because of him I'd come so close to becoming a wolfskin rug.

Something ugly and black rose up from deep inside me. I felt my power flow out like rising steam. I wanted to raise my head to the sky and howl in anger and frustration and loss. But I didn't. Instead, I let that rage rise up and carry me away on its red tide, reaching down deep inside to embrace the beast I'd become.

Ranger tried to say something, but the sound of it was drowned out by the sound of my own power roaring in my ears. I felt that wrenching sensation rip through me. Pain, but not quite, as my muscles and bones stretched and shifted. I felt my fingers shorten and my nails turn into claws. My ears popped, and my hearing was suddenly painfully sharp. So sharp I could almost hear the fur growing out of my skin. My insides did their gymnastics, and the dizzy sensation hit me, but passed quickly.

The minute I could move again, I loped a few paces back from the window, then launched. My sleek wolf body crashed through the glass in a smooth arc. I barely noticed the small cuts from the shattered glass. With a thud, I landed in Stephen's living room, teeth bared, hackles raised, and a growl of hatred low in my throat.

Stephen whirled around to face me. I felt rather than saw Ranger carefully step through the broken window into the living room.

Stephen looked in horror from Ranger back to me. "Is this Luc?" he asked in a harsh whisper.

I growled louder and took a step closer.

He backed up, bumping into the couch behind him.

"Tsk, tsk, tsk." Ranger's voice came from behind me. "Betraying someone else to the abolitionists? Surely you weren't arranging for the murder of any more Lycanthians. Or family members."

"Monsters aren't family," Stephen spat out. "And killing monsters isn't murder."

"Except to the other monsters." Ranger took another step forward. "Is that how you justified betraying Kennet? He was a monster, so his life didn't count?"

I growled again, louder. My anger rose until all I could feel was a red pounding in my brain.

"I betrayed Kennet because he killed my sister."

Everything inside me froze as those words hung in the air. A sickening scramble began in my gut. I turned to look at Ranger.

"He wasn't going to kill her," Ranger snarled back at Stephen. "He was going to turn her into a Lycanthian. That was the only way to keep the cancer from killing her. Lycanthians don't die from human diseases. If Kennet had lived long enough to turn Sara into a Lycanthian, she would be alive right now. Not only did your betrayal kill Kennet, but you denied your sister any chance at life."

So not only had Stephen betrayed my father to his death, but my mother as well.

I wanted him dead.

Without thinking further than that, I launched myself at Stephen with a low growl. The force of my blow took him over the arm of the couch, and we landed on the floor. I stood above him, my paws planted on his chest, my jaw wrapped around his neck, my teeth pressed against his jugular.

I stared into Stephen's blue eyes, so wide with fright that the whites showed all around them. He was breathing hard, and I could smell his fear.

It fed my anger. His fear made me feel powerful. I owned him in that moment. Whether he lived or died, it was my choice.

Between my jaws, under a very thin layer of skin, I felt Stephen's blood pulsing through his veins. Warm, salty blood, the very essence of life, pumping through him, mine for the taking.

Vengeance.

I remembered the deer we had hunted, how his life had seeped out of him.

No. The word rippled through my head, a soft cool breeze of reason in the midst of a red haze.

I pushed the word aside, wanting to sink my sharp teeth into his soft, weak flesh and stop that life with one swift motion of my jaw.

No. Louder this time.

A vision of Stephen's eyes, dull with death, flashed in my mind, and a sharp bite of grief punched through me. Slowly, like a ray of sun burning through a thick fog, I realized I didn't want to see Stephen dead.

What I really wanted was to turn back time, bring my family back, erase the hatred that had claimed so many lives. I wanted to make sure Stephen never bothered us again. And mostly, I didn't want to become what he was.

Killing him wouldn't bring my father back. It would only prove I had become the hideous beast he claimed I was, and claimed my father had been. If I didn't kill him, I would prove that he was a bigger monster than I was. He would have to live with that for the rest of his life.

Maybe that was an even greater justice.

I pulled back from that red haze, the hardest thing I've ever done. But I would not kill him. Instead, I pressed my fangs into the soft tissue of his neck, but gently. Just enough to leave four small punctures. They barely even bled, but I felt a warmth spread out on the lower part of Stephen's body, and the sharp scent of urine filled the air. He'd pissed his pants. In fear. Of me.

And in that moment, that was enough. I stepped away from him, a quivering, cowardly thing trying to pretend he was human. I knew he was nothing but a wretched beast.

My anger seeped from my body and emptied out of me in a swirling motion, like water escaping through a drain. I wasn't surprised to find myself back in human form. I looked down to where my uncle lay on the floor. "Always remember that, Stephen. I had your life between my jaws, and I stopped. Let those four scars remind you that you are a bigger monster than my father ever was. You will never escape that."

I stepped back. "Now, get up off the floor and swear you'll never try to find us or send anyone after us again."

Stephen scrambled back a few feet, and the distance made him reckless. "Why? What makes you think I'll do what you say?"

I stared at him, long and hard. What is the worst thing to happen to someone like Stephen? Worse even than death. Slowly, a smile spread across my face. "Think about it. I just sank my fangs into you."

He lifted his hand to the four small wounds I had just given him. When he pulled his fingers away, there was blood on them.

I leaned forward, towering over him. "I just *infected* you, *Uncle*. At the next full moon, guess what you'll be looking at in the mirror."

I had no idea if this was true or not, but I was hoping Stephen knew even less than me. I was also hoping Ranger would keep his mouth shut and let me play out the bluff. If it was a bluff.

Comprehension and horror spread across Stephen's face.

"What do you think is going to happen when your buddies find out you're a werewolf? Huh? You might just need a place to hide."

"Don't count on it. I'd rather die than turn into what you are."

"That can be arranged," Ranger said.

Stephen ignored that. "Besides, what makes you think I'm not going to pick up the phone the minute you leave here and let them know where you are?"

Ranger cocked his head to the side, as if examining some unusual specimen. "I'm curious. How did you plan to do it this time? I stopped using traceable license plates on my car right after you used Kennet's to betray him to the abolitionists."

"I don't need your license-plate number." Stephen looked smug for the first time since we'd arrived. That made me nervous. "Luc's cell phone has a GPS tracking device. They'll be able to track you . . ." He frowned as a realization struck him. "B-but they should have traced you here . . ."

"We got rid of the phone a long time ago. Besides, as Luc said, very soon, you're going to need someplace to hide. Do you really want your friends to know where that is?" Ranger turned to me. "Are you done here?"

"Yes," I said. "Almost. Where's Aunt Jane?" I asked Stephen. "I'm not ever coming back here, and I'd like to say good-bye."

"She left," Stephen said, his voice tight with anger. "Because of you."

I studied his lying face for a moment, then it hit me. "Not because of me! But because you were willing to betray me!" Aunt Jane had truly cared for me. That at least had been real.

Then, before I could start crying or anything dumb like that, I walked to the broken window and stepped back out into the night.

Ranger caught up to me and gave me a quick unreadable look before he got into the car.

I climbed in as well and fastened my seat belt, then started to shake. With relief. With fear. I'd come so close to killing someone tonight. I loved being this strong, having this kind of power and strength, but it was addictive, and it scared the spit out of me.

"Are you okay?" Ranger asked, his face concerned.

"Yeah. I guess." I turned to Ranger, my face set in grim lines. "I couldn't kill him, and if that makes me less of a werewolf, well, I can't help that."

"Refusing to kill Stephen doesn't make you less of a Lycanthian," Ranger said. "It makes you one who honors your code of protecting humans, a thinking one who puts his oath before his personal satisfaction. That makes you an ideal Lycanthian." He smiled, then started the car.

A warm feeling began in the pit of my stomach at his words, and I relaxed a bit. I might be only a half-breed, half Lycanthian and half human, but it was beginning to look like I'd gotten the good half of both. I turned to Ranger. "So," I asked, "*does* a shape-shifter bite turn humans into Lycanthians?"

I saw him grin, the light of the streetlamp flashing against his white teeth. "No. But it was a good bluff."

I smiled as I settled back into my seat. "Then how *do* you turn people into Lycanthians?"

"That's not something you have earned the right to know," Ranger said quietly. "Not just you," he hurried to explain as I started to protest, "but all juveniles. It is not knowledge to be treated lightly. When you become a fully adult pack member, then you will have the right to know."

We Lycanthians sure had a carload of secrets. As Ranger pulled out into the street, I turned for one final look at the place where I'd grown up.

Somewhere deep in the back of my mind I'd always thought that if things didn't work out with Ranger, I could come back here to live. If I ended up not liking my new life, I would be able to step back into my old one. I mean, I knew that Stephen and I would have had some serious making up to do, but I'd always thought the possibility was there. Like a safety net.

Now, next to the deep hole in my chest where my parents should have been, was another hole. The one where my old life used to be.

"What is it, Luc?" Ranger's voice gently interrupted my thoughts.

"That's the end of my old life. I can never go back. Ever."

Ranger didn't speak until he'd navigated the car out into the traffic and we were under way. Keeping his eyes on the road in front of him, he finally answered. "We Lycanthians have a saying. It comes from being chased from our homes so often throughout the centuries. We say that there are no endings in life, only new beginnings."

At his words, my shaking stopped and I grew calm. This wasn't the end. It was a new beginning, and I could live with that.

My total exhaustion caught up with me, and within seconds the soft sounds of the tires rolling along the highway lulled me to sleep. In my dreams, I ran beside the car, faster and faster until I was nothing but a blur of power and motion. I felt a presence beside me and turned my head. Another wolf ran with me. His fur was somewhere between gray and black, his eyes a striking brilliant green, just like mine, and when he turned to look at me, his strong noble face was full of pride.

He smelled of love and strength and home.

As we ran, he lifted his head and howled to the moon, letting the pack know we were coming home. For good.